POLEAXED

This book started to be written in 2018 and was finished in the summer of 2019, long before the current outbreak of the coronavirus, COVID-19. Any resemblance between the events described in this book and those following the COVID-19 pandemic is largely coincidental, but the measures put in place to prevent and treat all infectious diseases share common features, as do the mental sequelae.

POLEAXED

Peter Tyrer

The Book Guild Ltd

First published in Great Britain in 2020 by
The Book Guild Ltd
9 Priory Business Park
Wistow Road, Kibworth
Leicestershire, LE8 0RX
Freephone: 0800 999 2982
www.bookguild.co.uk
Email: info@bookguild.co.uk
Twitter: @bookguild

Typeset in 11pt Adobe Garamond Pro

Printed on FSC accredited paper
Printed and bound in Great Britain by 4edge Limited

ISBN 978 1913551 117

British Library Cataloguing in Publication Data.
A catalogue record for this book is available from the British Library.

Dedicated to all those sufferers who feel
they have been misdiagnosed

Preliminary note:

Parity of esteem is the principle by which mental health must be given equal priority to physical health. It was enshrined in law by the Health and Social Care Act, 2012.

Has it happened? Will it ever happen? Read on.

ONE

DAY ONE, FOUR CASES, ONE DEATH

*A time there was – as one may guess, before the birth of
consciousness, when all went well*

Thomas Hardy, 1901

Barbara Dukinfield had never had so much attention in
her nineteen years of existence. More would follow, but
currently she was barely conscious and any appreciation she
may have had was marred. The first four cases of the Poleaxe
Syndrome had just been brought to Medenby Hospital. It
was a mysterious disease that paralysed the arms and legs
so quickly that its victims fell down on the spot. Barbara
was one of them, brought directly from Central Park in the
town by a nervous ambulance crew who had been advised
to don protective clothing and to avoid contact with the
people carrying this unknown affliction. The nurses were
equally hesitant, told clearly by Matron Arbuthnot to treat
this condition as a virulent infection and to wear masks at
all times. Barbara's lithe but lifeless body was lifted gently

1

onto the special mattress covering the iron bedstead and the curtains drawn carefully. The notice 'Poleaxe Case' was pinned at the foot of the bed and the nurses moved quietly away.

Barbara did not want the doors to open in the long dark corridor of her mind. But she had to open them a little, just a little. Too much and she would be dazzled, and that was truly awful. So she opened them a little, crack by crack. What was there? First it was the music. Melodious, penetrating and insistent. Barbara listened without understanding, then was jolted towards consciousness. She was part of what was going on. But could she influence it, and was it real? She slowly opened her eyes. There was a white ridge a short distance away in the landscape. What was it? She closed her eyes again.

The music had stopped and in its place she heard murmuring. Like the noise of flowing water. Now that was familiar. She was back on the banks of the Haggins, down in the valley close to the village and her home, surrounded by those friendly trees, the alders, with their rod-straight branches, their roots greedy, thrusting and lusting towards the water in the stream. Above, their shiny dimpled leaves gathered together to make an arbour overhead; between the branches the dappled sun created gentle patterns below. Tickling the water with her fishing rod with a juicy worm for bait, she startled the trout in the deeper pools, and the crayfish grumbled in the muddy shallows as their peace was disturbed. This was where she wanted to be; this was home.

But the murmuring was changing. It was no longer the reassuring sound of water. There were harsher noises. They were changing. Into voices. Barbara wanted not to hear but something told her she must. But it was very hard and the words just floated like gossamer in and around her head.

'This Poleaxe is serious, always wear your masks and gloves.'

'Mole pats to cheer us,' Barbara translated. 'What fun, Harry the mole there too, with his neat little pats round the fishing place.' This was exciting. Barbara wanted to clap her hands.

'Mr Craske must be moved to the post-mortem room immediately.'

'Ask for love in the post-autumn room, how romantic,' translated Barbara.

'Please keep a check on all their breathing. It begins to fail when they get ascending paralysis.'

'Sending palaces too,' trilled the voice in Barbara's mid-brain. That would be a real joy, down by the river. Eating the fish in sumptuous splendour. She did not want this feeling to stop.

But something forced her to listen more carefully. The voice carried authority. Someone responded.

'Yes, of course, Matron. This is nerve-wracking, but I'm experienced in treating patients in isolation. It's different for the nursing assistants. Some of them feel these precautions are a bit of a joke.'

'Well, impress on them immediately: this disease is a medical emergency, and they are on the front line. And, by the way, you must check the fluid balance of that new case, Dukinfield, she may need a drip.'

Barbara was startled. Dukinfield, that was her name. Why were they talking about her? How annoying to be interrupted. She was still fishing in the stream. The noises moved away and she could resume her game by the water.

But something had broken the memory trace. Her mind was fuzzy, still full of porridgy distractions, but she was being forced back to the present. She must open her eyes again and focus. Wasn't that a new shape breaking the uniformity of the white background? Narrowing her eyes, she saw a figure moving slowly a few feet away. It was grey rather than white. It shuffled and had a curious head with a long nose. She was startled. This must be an animal of some sort. Yes, it was. It was a donkey. Her thoughts were buzzing. She remembered her grandmother telling her about the time of death. When people died, and if for some reason were brought back to life, all they remembered was a sea of bright white light. A vision of heaven. But not a donkey. Yet, as her father kept reminding her, Jesus took his final journey to Jerusalem on a donkey. Was she on her last journey too?

She opened her eyes a little wider. That white ridge was a very short distance away now. Try and work it out. Yes, when she breathed more deeply and slowly, the ridge moved up and down in unison. Of course, bedsheets. What else was she able to control? Her eyes and ears seemed to be working well, but what about her arms and legs? Now she was getting alarmed. She could see them and feel them in an eerie sort of way, but they were detached. She could not move them. They were dead. Did they belong to her, or somebody else? As everything in her life had been turned upside down, their ownership was in question.

Her memory was still hazy. But someone had said 'Dukinfield'. That was the key. The Dukinfield she knew

4

had been having a sandwich in the park. But what had happened to her? She was walking across the park and next was on the ground. Then she was in this bed, just like that. But was this other Dukinfield the same as her, or just an interfering interloper?

Before she could decide the answer to this fundamental question, she was interrupted. Another shape was casting a shadow over her. It was like the donkey she had seen earlier, with a long face. But, on opening her eyes wider, this shape was clearly human. It had a duck bill mask where the mouth should have been, but a neat, finely embroidered butterfly cap on the head above.

'Good morning, Barbara,' said a muffled voice behind the mask. 'I am Nurse Grant and I would like you to try and pass some water.' She produced what appeared to be a large, squashed metal teapot. Why was this stranger interrupting her dreams?

'But I have already passed the water – it was quite lovely.'

'I'm sure it was,' said Nurse Grant as she hoisted Barbara up in a swift, practised movement and placed the squashed teapot under her bottom. Barbara startled as she felt the cold metal touch her buttocks. But she was certainly awake now. She was firmly and unequivocally in the world of the hospital ward.

TWO

DAY TWO, FIVE CASES, ONE DEATH

*There is nothing more difficult to carry out, nor more
doubtful of success, nor more dangerous to handle, than to
initiate a new order of things*

Niccolo Machiavelli, 1513

James studied himself in front of the bedroom mirror.
Studied, not admired. But admiration was not far off. He
was looking at a man with thick dark hair, forty-five years
old, with interesting stubble round his cheek and chin,
square face with jutting jaw, and a strong, firm mouth. A
striking appearance, just short of handsome, he thought.
Yes, the striped shirt, plus cufflinks, was best for today,
with a plain red bow tie to show his political affiliations.
James was taking time to ensure he was in the best shape to
face William Fothergill, the medical director of Medenby
Hospital, who was known to be a snappy dresser. He was
determined not to be intimidated by William, and in the
dress stakes at the beginning they must start as equal.

He saw Snow reflected in the mirror, lying on the bed, stretched out as though on a rack, but this was not the right metaphor, as he was just getting comfortable and needed a great space for rapture. Snow was a paradoxical cat. He was black all over but had four white paws and a triangle of white on his chest. James liked being asked why he was called Snow, as he could then introduce his speech about John Snow, who, with his demonstration of the source of cholera at the Broad Street Pump in 1854, was the instigator of the public health revolution in England. The development of good sanitation, clean water and positive hygiene had saved thousands of lives. But Snow only had a few patches of white. Ah yes, that was true; it showed that public health still had a long way to go, so most of Snow still remained black.

James had finished in his boudoir.

'Off for breakfast,' he said to Snow, who, after a short pause to demonstrate his independence, trotted down the stairs after him. Elaine, always efficient, had anticipated his arrival and, just as he arrived in the kitchen, took out his boiled egg, placed it in the patterned wooden egg cup that James had been given in Norway some years ago, together with hot buttered toast. Snow jumped on his lap temporarily to show that he still mattered.

They both listened to the radio. Yes, the news was exciting. Another case of the so-called Poleaxe Syndrome had been identified in their town. Sir George Gribbins, the Chief Medical Officer to the government, had considered it important enough to make a reassuring comment to the public, but this only added to the drama.

Medenby was now on the map of national consciousness; no longer a small town somewhere in the East Midlands that all could unthinkingly pass by. Of course it was troubling that there were other cases of this syndrome, first identified in Medenby just over a week ago, but to him it was a welcome opportunity. As Medical Officer of Health for the town, one of James's main responsibilities was to prevent the spread of infectious diseases should they arise.

As it was likely that an infective agent was the cause of the Poleaxe Syndrome, he should be the one tasked with bringing it under control. Some would say 'could' rather than 'should', but in James's view this was his responsibility, as the public health expert, to take on. But it was a completely new syndrome, or so they said, so it would be a major challenge to his skills and acumen. Of course the task would require the help of many others, and he would have to figure a way of achieving this. He was used to being in charge of a small unit, giving orders to his staff of six, knowing they would be followed to the letter. This new challenge was far bigger. He would have to use diplomatic skills, not always on full display, and would have to try and control his temper, which often flared at inconvenient times.

He reviewed his plan as he drove to the hospital – grinding through the gears unnecessarily – and had a surge of rewarding anger. Those self-satisfied bastards at medical school who made fun of him when he said he would specialise in public health would get their comeuppance.

'Public health,' they sneered. 'That's not a real job. Sending letters to people to get vaccinated and counting cases of VD. Should be called pubic health.'

He would show them. Public health was more than important; it was absolutely essential to public safety. It should never be relegated to the back of medicine.

He threaded his car along the inner road that passed alongside the many buildings that together made up Medenby Hospital. Of course, it was not really a hospital at all. It started life as a workhouse and, despite many refurbishments, makeovers and long, antiseptic corridors, it still shouted 'workhouse' to the people who entered its large grounds.

The workhouses were a regular feature of the Victorian landscape. James had learnt much about them in his training. The first Medical Officer of Health was appointed 120 years ago and their duties involved supervising conditions at the workhouses. These were terrible at the time. Women, men and children were all separated, despised and underfed, wearing shapeless uniforms that robbed their identities, and the work prescribed to 'protect them from indolence' was callous and brutal.

'Collecting oakum' sounded reasonable, but as it involved separating tarry ropes and extracting every fibre with bare hands, leaving them filthy and bruised, it was an ugly task. The workers were also involved in bone-crushing to make fertiliser, but when fights broke out between the men stripping the meat off putrid bones to stave off hunger, even this could not be tolerated, and the practice soon stopped. James was proud that his predecessors in public health had helped to reform these places of systematic abuse and eventually promote their closure. But the buildings remained as a stark memory of the past.

But James could see advantages in this old architecture. The dull, squat red Victorian buildings were ideal for treating people who needed isolation from others, and they might all be needed if this Poleaxe Syndrome became an epidemic.

The ward staff were expecting him. The five patients with the Poleaxe Syndrome were all in a side ward normally used for overspill patients. Because of the likelihood the syndrome might be infectious, the nurses were adopting standard control practice. The patients were set in beds apart from the others, each curtained off, and each nurse was gowned and wearing a mask, all of different types, some looking comfortable and efficient, others lumbering about as though they had picked the wrong uniform. James observed them from the nursing station in the corner of the ward. He was waiting for the matron and Dr Giles Camberwell, the junior doctor attached to the ward, to arrive.

As James watched, he was surprised how quiet it was. The nurses flitted about from bed to bed, pulling aside curtains and then drawing them again, and their muffled voices through their masks hardly registered. There was a general air of foreboding and dread mixed with disinfectant; it was surreal. James was taken back in time to his first experience of the dissecting room as a medical student. Yes, of course on that occasion the subjects were all dead. The students knew what to expect. But, even so, when they encountered these stiff white bodies, surrounded by the stench of formalin, they were silent, nervous and discomfited. They shuffled around looking for the bodies and the parts to which they had been allocated – head and neck, leg, arm, abdomen – it was all very bizarre and off-putting. Although it was not long before the usual student wisecracks and facetious interruptions softened the tension – 'Where's the left side of this body? Don't worry, it's all right now' – at the beginning all were subdued.

The nurses here seemed similarly nervous and unsettled, and for good reason. They approached the patients in the beds with the same combination of reluctance and trepidation that James remembered as a student. Perhaps the similarities were stronger than might at first appear, but, of course, here there was added danger. For all the nurses knew, the charges under their care could all be dead within the week, and, if they erred in protecting themselves, they might also follow them to the grave. But despite the tension, James was invigorated. He was now at a critical point in his career. He wasn't being corny, but he knew that he was a man who had skills as a detective, communicator and inspirational leader. This was the chance to exercise them. The first task was to be a detective.

Dr Camberwell came into the nursing station. They greeted each other. James looked him over.

'I haven't met a medical officer of health before. This is going to be a new experience.'

'Are not we all medical officers of health? But you are going to have to get used to this new one. I think you're going to see quite a lot of me in the next few weeks.'

They were interrupted. Matron Miriam Arbuthnot arrived. But 'arrived' was hardly the right word. It was a visitation. She swept into the office with a derisory look at James, clearly an alien in her domain. An Amazon in nurse's clothing. He could imagine her lifting fifteen-stone men out of bed on her own, carrying a mattress under each arm, a juggernaut cutting through every obstruction. With her long, unsmiling face and starched pristine white and blue uniform, she forced respect and attention. James and the two men, neither of them insignificant, seemed small beside her. Dr Camberwell, as a relatively new doctor, was intimidated by her presence and could only stammer his name as he introduced himself.

Miriam turned to James. 'Ah, you must be Dr Porting, the public health chappie.' Miriam frequently tried to soften her public image by descending to the vernacular.

'Dr Porton, actually,' said James. He was irritated but was forcing himself to stay on the right side of this particular dragon. He was going to need an ally.

'Sorry, never was very good on names; I think they said I was dysloxic at school. But what can I do for you gentlemen? As you can see, we are rather busy.'

James noted the ward did not seem to be busy at all, but still nodded. 'We need to know as much as possible about the Poleaxe cases, Matron, from the public health perspective.'

'I'll try to help, but do remember, my perspective is the hospital one, so I don't want you bothering my gels any more than necessary. They have clear instructions and "do not be diverted from your tasks" is one of them. Until we know what is going on with this disease we must regard it as a killer, waiting to infect everybody with whom it comes into contact'.

James thought she was probably exaggerating, but it was important for him to agree with her.

'Matron, we do very much appreciate your time and help. Our intention is to stay out of your way, but at the same time – with your help, of course – try as much as we can to find the cause of this very worrying syndrome. As it is so new, we must examine every clue to its origin.'

Miriam had spent enough time. 'You can rely on my nurses to keep me informed, and I am sure that Dr

Camberwell here will do so too. Thank you, Dr Portent, for your visit. But we must understand each other. I follow my mentor, Florence Nightingale, in my motto, "good nursing needs discipline". So if you follow the rules, and always sterilise your hands and wear the right protective clothing, you are welcome here. If you break these rules, I will spare you nothing and banish you for good.' She gave a hollow laugh. James and Giles were not certain if her comment might be interpreted as a joke. But her fixed stare afterwards showed it clearly was not.

Oily James responded before Angry James could collect his thoughts. 'Of course, Matron. We are on the same wavelength. If we work together and join our skills in unison we can understand, and beat, this disease. We will keep you abreast of our findings and hope the staff here can keep us abreast of theirs.'

'Good.' Miriam swivelled and left as dramatically as she had arrived. But her words has struck home. She was as formidable in her absence as she was in their presence. Florence Nightingale would have been proud of her acolyte.

James relaxed, but he had to make the most of Giles Camberwell while they were together. Giles was going to be on the front line of his Poleaxe investigation. He was going to be assessing all the patients as they arrived and must be cultivated.

'Dr Camberwell, or can I call you Giles?'

'I'm happy with Giles. My folks all come from New Zealand, where we don't bother with second names.'

'Good. I take it you have seen all the five patients with the Poleaxe Syndrome so far?'

'Yeah. They all got moved to the side ward once it was clear the problem was muscle paralysis.'

'And have you taken full histories from all of them? Is there anything that might link them together?'

James was desperate to find links in the onset of the disease. These were the key to solving the problem.

'No, it's all a bit odd. We first admitted Fred Entwistle, a bell-ringer in the parish church. He collapsed in the belfry, high up in Medenby Parish Church, in the middle of bell-ringing. It was quite a task getting him out of the church. They had to put him in a large bag to protect his paralysed arms and legs and take him down the spiral stone steps a hundred feet to the ground. Next there was Gordon Craske, who was collecting his pension and travelled through the park on his way home. At least we think so, but as he died from ascending paralysis two days after admission and never properly recovered consciousness, we cannot be certain. His was the first death and we all felt terrible as we could do nothing about it. The third was Barbara Dukinfield, who lost consciousness in the park after having a sandwich – nice girl, you can see her over there.' Giles gestured to the nearest bed.

'Then we admitted Julia Unwincroft, she's fifty-five and came back to her house in Medenby from Singapore three weeks ago. She collapsed outside the public library in Beamish Gardens. She still hasn't recovered consciousness sufficiently to talk properly. Finally the last two, just admitted, Mary Beckinsale and Henry Carpenter, both in their forties, were found close to the Palace Theatre in Applegate. They are too unwell to be interviewed properly at present.'

'That's a good summary,' said James. 'Now I would like to set you a task. I hope it's not too difficult. Can you find out what all of them were doing in the day or so before they collapsed and whether anything was common to them all? I mean anything. It could be what they had eaten or drunk, where they had been, what they had been doing and lots more. And, if you find anything that is universally common, could you' – here James pulled out a scruffy notepad from his jacket pocket and tore a sheet off – 'could you telephone me at my office or at home on this number?'

He wrote it down and handed it to Giles, who was interested and unfazed.

'I get it. You're looking for a sequence, and then a cause. I think I can help to do that for you.'

'Just one more thing. If you can find out anything in the next few hours, it would be a great help. I'm seeing the medical director late in the afternoon and need to be reinforced with as much information as possible.'

'Fair enough.' Giles too was interested in being the detective's assistant. This would be a new role, and an interesting one, for a junior doctor with a penchant to learn in the middle of a crisis.

THREE

DAY TWO, FIVE CASES, ONE DEATH

A defender must always seek to change over to the attack as soon as he has gained the benefit of the defence

Carl von Clausewitz, 1832

James had to move quickly. He had his assistant, Giles, in place, and now it was time to see the senior people who would also need to be on his side. It was not going to be automatic, but he was determined to lead the Poleaxe investigation. Medical officers of health were often side-lined but, even though epidemics like this were rare, all their training prepared them for this eventuality. The chance would be unlikely to come again, so he must gird up all his courage if he was going to lead the way.

This was why his interview with William Fothergill, the senior physician at Medenby Hospital, was going to be so important. William regarded himself as a natural leader. James had to persuade him that on this occasion James needed to take over. It really was a non-starter. A hospital consultant with little knowledge of the community was ill-placed to investigate a condition that was being played out away from his familiar doorstep.

He parked close to the main building. His feet scrunched the gravel as he walked up the path and entered the reception.

'Could I see Dr Fothergill? I have a planned appointment with him.'

The receptionist, a girl not long out of school, looked at him quizzically. 'I'm sorry. I don't know who you are, sir. Whom shall I say has called?'

'Tell him Dr Porton is here,' James replied irritably. He had expected to be recognised, even though he seldom had reason to come into the hospital. But it would be different now.

'Thank you, Dr Porton, could you take a seat.' The girl intimated where with a flick of her head. She was not going to be intimidated.

Within minutes, Dr William Fothergill appeared, urbane, smooth and well-groomed.

'Ah, Porton, nice to see you again. Please do come in.' James grimaced; these ex-public-school doctors never remembered first names.

William and James entered the well-manicured room with its imposing leather armchair behind the solid mahogany desk. James could not help noticing a photograph of the large Fothergill family as he sat down, reminding him of his own absence of progeny.

William leant forward conspiratorially. 'I can see why you're here – it's the Poleaxe cases, isn't it?'

'Yes.'

'What's your take on it?'

James took a deep breath. He must be firm and confident, but not aggressive. 'I have to start out with the premise that this is an infectious disease. Obviously, nobody can be certain yet, but if this is one and we ignore it, we could well have an epidemic on our hands. It may already be occurring. There are lots of pointers. The disease appears to come from a single source that then affected others; at least, that is how Dr Camberwell sees it. I also understand that people with the syndrome have fevers, and there are blood changes that are non-specific but are consistent with infection.'

William nodded, slowly but doubtfully.

'But there are other explanations, and I, in my position, have to consider them all. The syndrome is not all that different from drop attacks when there is a temporary loss of blood to the brain; it has some odd, abnormal signs and some overlap with multiple sclerosis and encephalitis, and, of course, we can never forget the simulators.'

'The simulators?'

'You know, the phoney syndromes. They look good, smell good, but test wrong. Especially the favourite of our mental health friends, mass hysteria. When we get that wrong, they all have a good belly laugh.'

'But if this is an infection and, as seems likely, it spreads quickly, we could have hundreds of cases and many deaths if we fail to take proper precautions.'

William smiled. 'You foresee doom too readily, Porton. So, assuming you are right, what do you suggest?'

This was the opening James needed. 'We have to approach this in the same way as typhoid. Assume everyone

18

with the syndrome is infectious, isolate them in separate wards, use barrier nursing to avoid infecting staff, and take specimens from every orifice – for culture, microscopy and immunology.'

'Why do you think it is the same as typhoid?'

'I have no idea if it is like typhoid. What I do know,' and here James raised his voice to make his point absolutely clear, 'that if the Poleaxe Syndrome is like typhoid, and we ignore it, the consequences will be disastrous. As you well know, the recent typhoid epidemic in Aberdeen in 1964 went from a few cases to four hundred within the space of two weeks. If Poleaxe is similar, and we have no treatment for it, there could be mass fatalities.'

William mused a little, then his eyes brightened and he looked up.

'Well, let us not get too excited, and remember there were no fatalities in Aberdeen, although I note we have had one already here. But we have anticipated you to some extent, and all the Poleaxe cases are being treated in isolation at present, as I agree here we cannot be over-cautious. Perhaps can we come to a working arrangement. If we regard the Poleaxe Syndrome as a possible infection and admit all the patients to Block G, then others to Block H if the ward becomes full, sealing both units from the rest of the hospital, then we can accommodate your concerns and investigate the disease in closer detail. It is perfectly proper for you, as Medical Officer of Health, to oversee the public health aspects of this, but you must leave the investigations and other enquiries to our medical and laboratory teams.'

James was about to interrupt as he could see his influence leaking away, but then he realised he had been offered a way forward. 'Agreed, Dr Fothergill. All I ask is to be the spokesman for the public. After all, my responsibility is to keep the population of Medenby informed and it is only right that they are kept fully in the picture. We cannot allow panic to take over.'

William intimated the meeting was over by slowly rising to his feet, smiling with a touch of condescension. James both resented and admired him in equal measure. His supreme self-confidence James could never hope to emulate, but his open scorn for others who were less well-endowed rankled long and deep.

'That's settled then. I'll make sure that Blocks G and H are reconstituted as an isolation unit and we will admit all cases of the Poleaxe Syndrome to G or H at the discretion of the senior nurses. Matron Arbuthnot is in her element here. She loves a challenge like this and will make sure that every precaution is taken. I can guarantee that every nurse working will be "Arbuthnot approved". We still have some nurses who nursed diphtheria cases years ago. They'll be keen to get back into mode.'

James rose from his chair, satisfied. Now the final thrust. 'I'll let all know in our department. We'll set up a Poleaxe Task Group to monitor progress. I hope we can have it at the hospital and that you can join it too.'

'Of course. We must all be part of the problem, and of the solution.'

James walked out, triumphant. His suggestion of a Poleaxe Task Group had been agreed without demur and the wording of his last sentence showed that he could lead the group. The Poleaxe investigation would be Porton's investigation. He left through reception, head held higher than when he came in, and could not help feel the insolent girl at the desk was now showing him more respect. This meeting had gone better than he expected. The next step was to inform Radio Medenby.

FOUR

DAY TEN, FORTY-FIVE CASES, THREE DEATHS

But human experience is usually paradoxical,
that means incongruous with the phrases of current
talk or even current philosophy

George Eliot, 1876

Barbara was getting better quickly, faster than anyone else on the ward. The events outside, with a rapid increase in cases of Poleaxe leading people close to panic, were being kept from her and everybody else in Block G. 'Don't do anything to raise their excitement, gels,' Matron Arbuthnot had told her nurses. 'Blissful ignorance does no harm.'

But Barbara was already getting bored. Lying in bed for all but one hour each day was a bore. Having nothing to do was a bore. Isolation was becoming a threat; it led to rumination and uncertainty. Unnecessary rumination about herself, her mortality, her insignificant place in the world. This was not helping her recovery, as it made her doubt. And doubt was the fuel that fed her continuous anxiety.

The curtains round the bed were now a brick wall, keeping the world out and fencing her in, almost like a criminal. Of course, anyone could persuade her that this was nonsense, but at this sensitive point in her life impressions were all, and she could not dismiss the idea that she must have erred in some way to be placed in this position. Superstitions abounded. Was this mysterious syndrome a punishment for past misdeeds? Where had she gone wrong in life? Why was she now isolated in a place having all the threat and impersonality of a prison cell?

The bell rang for visiting time. Good. Something new was happening. She could lose her anxious dread and foreboding. Who would be coming today? She listened carefully. Then she heard footsteps: rapid, perhaps someone even running. Was that allowed in the ward? Then, whoever it was was outside. She could see shiny brown shoes below the curtain.

'Sorry I'm not allowed to see you properly today, sis. You can probably guess why. It's 'cos I'm infectious today, as you can probably tell. Quite a joke, really. Both infectious, both spreading germs, both out of bounds.'

Barbara liked the throaty male voice and wanted to hear more but felt she ought to reply.

But he continued. 'Got something for you too. You must be bored stiff on your own in that bed. Read this, and you're bound to cheer up.'

A hand appeared round the end of the bed and a book was deposited on her bedside table.

'I'm very sorry, but I think you must have got the wrong person. My name is Barbara Dukinfield.' She stopped, annoyed with herself for sounding so prissy. There was a short silence.

'Well, well, I am sorry, Barbara. My sister's here somewhere; they must have moved her. I'm Danny, nice to meet you, even if it's only a curtain call.'

He laughed and coughed at the same time. 'Hope to see you again some time – properly, that is.'

'Yes, but you must take your book back for your sister.'

'OK.'

But then there was a pause.

'Tell you what. You read it first and when you've finished I can see you again and pass it on to my sister. I know she wouldn't mind.'

'That's very kind and generous. You've really cheered me up today.'

'Good. Thanks for the chat. Must find my sister now.'

The shoes disappeared from the bottom of the curtain and the steps faded.

Barbara was ridiculously overwhelmed. The last few minutes were really quite exciting. But nothing had happened to make her feel like this. It was just a mistake. What was so special about a mistake? Was this a reaction to Poleaxe? Was her life starting over again?

Before she could answer these metaphysical questions, the curtains were drawn and there, still some distance away for health reasons, stood two people, erect, stiff, masked, gowned and looking macabre like extras in a poor horror film, the Reverend Robert and Mrs Pamela Dukinfield.

'Darling,' gushed Pamela. 'You're looking so much better today. Bit of colour back in your cheeks, I see.' She darted forward and pinched Barbara's cheek to ensure there would be colour there now, whatever existed before.

Barbara laughed. 'I feel like a time cleaner. I go around hoovering every second and minute up, then put them in the corner and can't remember for the life of me where I've put them. And now they're all gone.'

'Don't be so melodramatic, darling. It can't be that bad. Anyway, I see you've been reading.' She picked up the book left on the bedside table. '*Catch-22*. I've heard about this – bit on the edge, isn't it? Where on earth did you get this from?'

'It was left by a friend.'

'Friend? Now, that does sound interesting. Anyone we know?'

Barbara felt a looming barrage of interrogation, so to avoid it she lied. 'No, it was just one of the nurses on the ward. Thought the book might be of interest.'

She could hardly say anything more. She was clueless about its content. Fortunately her mother was diverted into matters of greater importance.

'We can't wait to get you back home, darling. I know it's going to take some time, but there's a lot that needs to be done and it can't be done without you. There's the recarpeting of your bedroom, the planning of the midsummer church outing, and, of course, the annual congregation whist drive, nobody else can organise that. And there are letters from your faculty at university. Had to open one of them. They wanted to know where you were and why you hadn't turned up for the new term.'

'Mum, how many times have I told you not to open my letters? I know I am in hospital, but I can deal with these myself.'

'But this was special, darling. I just had to tell them you were at death's door and couldn't possibly respond.'

Barbara felt her anxiety levels rise again to their normal high point. Mum could always be guaranteed to assist in raising her anxiety, even though she hadn't the slightest clue what she was doing. Whatever else happened when she left hospital, it would not be a time for recuperative leisure. But still, it was what she had expected: back to the normal routine as soon as possible, no allowance made. She found it easier to fall into line.

'OK, Mum. I'll do my best to help,' she replied in the little girly voice she always used on such occasions.

'But of course you need to be completely better first,' her father interjected, trying to offset the hardness of his wife's tone, but never quite compensating.

Barbara smiled, wanly but gratefully. Her father was an honourable lightweight: kind, well-meaning and godly, a continual leaven to his wife's harshness, but without the strength to properly oppose.

Pamela soldiered on. 'So we've seen Dr Camberwell, the registrar, and checked with Dr Porton, and, because you've done so well, discharge might be possible in the next few weeks, we understand, but only if all continues to go well. You'll have to be confined to home, but that won't bother you, will it? After all, you're a home-loving girl.'

'Yes, Mum. I'd like to be back home.' Barbara sounded pathetic – she was.

'Good, we're off now, lots of love. Back tomorrow, toodle-oo.' Pamela veered away, but not before lowering her head and giving Barbara a quick peck on the cheek via her mask in the same movement. Robert followed, dutifully.

Barbara was now both agitated and deflated. She couldn't understand why. Here she was in an environment that was antiseptic, sterile and boring. Time after time she had rehearsed her leaving. Dressed in clothes that followed the lines of her figure, not the shapeless gowns that made her look like a pantomime clown, she would walk with her shoulders straight, her head high, nodding gratefully to the staff as the door was opened and then, ecstatically, she could gulp those first breaths of fresh air on the way to the family Morris Minor Traveller, with its chunky, reassuring wooden frame cheerfully inviting her back into the family.

So why had this image retreated into the mist? Her anxiety was welling up again; she was jittery and restless and had to get out of bed and walk around. She struggled out of the bedclothes, walked past the two beds at the end of the ward, and suddenly knew no more.

FIVE

DAY TWELVE, SIXTY CASES, FOUR DEATHS

We need an assembly, not for cleverness,
but for setting things straight

William Golding, 1954

'This is Radio Medenby, your new local radio station. Local news, local interest. But the first item is also national news; the latest information about the Poleaxe Syndrome in the town? There are now sixty confirmed cases, all in the town. The patients are in the isolation wings of Medenby Hospital so we have been reassured the rest of us we are in no danger. A further statement will be made later today at 5pm by Dr Porton, Medical Officer of Health, who has kindly agreed to give daily bulletins on the progress of this disease on this station. Please keep in touch with Radio Medenby. We are the station to give you all the latest announcements.'

James listened with a mixture of approbation and mild annoyance. It was good to have his name broadcast to all, but he must have a word with the announcers about overstressing 'danger'; these sufferers were not criminals. And they were making too much of Radio Medenby, a tinpot organisation if ever there was one. But as he turned the radio off, he realised that Radio Medenby could be very helpful to him too. He must cultivate it more.

He manoeuvred his car into one of the parking places marked 'CONSULTANTS ONLY' by the main building. It had been agreed he could park there for the meetings of the Poleaxe Task Group. He was glad to be given the status of a consultant, if only by proxy. A small acknowledgement of his new status, but an important one.

He walked into the headquarters building and the Committee Room without being challenged. He was the first to arrive, so was able to place his attaché case at the end of the long mahogany table in preparation to chairing the meeting. He had planned it in some detail. There would be a lot of clever people coming. They would know considerably more than him about the more esoteric aspects of medicine, but if he was able to chair the meeting firmly, limit discussion and control the agenda, his limitations in knowledge would be dwarfed by his ability to grasp and synthesise the essentials.

The next to arrive was Madeleine Bishop, the senior health visitor in James's department. Madeleine was an ardent believer in health education and she was a frontline worker, not afraid of getting her hands dirty. James knew she would be important in controlling the spread of Poleaxe. It was not easy getting approval for Madeleine to join the group, but James was determined to have a reliable ally in the discussions, and he persuaded the others that education was going to be an essential element in his plans to control the epidemic, as he quite expected it to be, whatever others might think.

The other members of the group began to trickle in. Next to come was William Fothergill, who seemed to James to be irritated that he had not arrived first, as no doubt he felt the Committee Room was his domain.

Definitely not for this meeting, James said to himself.

The consultant neurologist, Charles Merridew, sauntered in. Charles was supremely self-confident, not just because he knew more than everyone else, but had the additional advantage, very annoying to James, of being ruggedly handsome. When people looked at official photographs of Medenby staff his was the one that always aroused comment, while James looked surly at the periphery.

'I do like the look of him,' said dozens of admiring women, before becoming silent and deferring further speech to dwell on fantasy. He kept himself fit by playing squash twice a week and was seldom reported to lose. His only unflattering feature was his creepily serpent smile, condescendingly shown when others failed to keep up with his scintillating intellect. James knew he would have to be very careful in managing Charles's contribution to the meeting. A combination of deference to his status and awe at his intellect would do very well.

James looked up. Dr Archibald Patterson, the pathologist, was next to arrive. He was another sticky one, a small, balding Scotsman with a silvery moustache, for whom the word 'dour' would have had to be invented if it did not already exist. Some people actually thought he had created the word as his second name was Dewar. He was diligent, pedantic and insufferably accurate, with an excellent memory. James viewed him with care, respect and disdain. He had to be respected for his knowledge and encyclopaedic brain, but he was impossibly irritating, and after one of his long soliloquys you could almost hear the gritting and grinding of teeth of those forced to listen, contrasting with the somnolence of others who had succumbed to torpor.

Despite these failings, James realised that he could keep Archie on his side by never interrupting him and always thanking him profusely.

Within minutes the rest of the Poleaxe Task Group had arrived: Miriam Arbuthnot, the matron, trained at the Florence Nightingale School of Nursing and who felt at all times that she was representing her illustrious mentor; Philip Boulton, the haematologist, whose expertise in blood disorders made his participation automatic; and Christopher Barclay, an all-round physician who could always be guaranteed to keep people's feet on the ground.

When all were seated, James coughed – it was a good way to create silence – and then he began, serious, determined, and unfazed.

'Thank you for coming today. We are faced with a health crisis in Medenby. It is of national, not just local importance. Our task is to make the people of this town safe, and we can only do this by understanding, by unlocking and, in the end, defeating, this condition called the Poleaxe Syndrome.'

James had rehearsed this preamble. He wanted a sombre beginning to prepare them for what would come later. He looked around. They were all sitting more upright than before. He had their attention, so he must capitalise on this.

'Are you happy with me chairing this meeting, William?' This was a key moment, and by using Dr Fothergill's first name, James sensed that agreement would be difficult to refuse.

'Yes, of course,' said William, just a little grudgingly.

'Good. Can we start with you, Dr Merridew? You have examined most of these cases. What are your initial conclusions?'

Charles Merridew stayed in his seat and drawled. People like Charles did not need to rise and could always drawl. He had a natural authority that inhibited interruption. 'Poleaxe is a very interesting disease. I believe it is primarily a neurological disorder – I will outline my reasons. First, there is hyper-reflexia, the overactivity you see in upper motor neuron lesions, but also paralysis indicative of lower motor neuron ones. A very unusual combination.'

'I am very sorry, Dr Merridew,' Madeleine interrupted. 'I am not a neurologist and cannot quite follow all of what you are saying. Are you saying it is like polio, or like a stroke?'

'That is the odd feature. It has elements of both – polio as a lower motor neurone disorder, stroke as an upper one. But there is another strange feature. The effects may become permanent, but they also have the capacity to fluctuate.'

It was clear to James that Charles was fascinated by the intellectual challenge of Poleaxe. This was good. Charles would be unlikely to interfere with the practical solutions that James already had in mind. So he could now move the discussion on.

'Thank you, Dr Merridew. That is an excellent start to our discussion, a very fluent summary. Can I ask you, Dr Patterson, with your wide expertise, to let us have your views about the possible pathology?'

Archibald Patterson rose slowly to his feet, which had little impact as it added little to his seated figure. He had a set of documents in front of him. This was clearly going to be a long haul.

'I have never seen anything like this in my laboratory before, so I do not understand this syndrome. My tests have failed to elucidate an answer.'

He continued to tell everybody, quite unnecessarily, about other conditions that he knew, but were unlike the Poleaxe Syndrome, and referred to his papers frequently. Eventually James had to interrupt.

'I think many of us here would like to know about the bacteriological findings. Have you been able to find anything abnormal?'

'I was about to come to that,' Archie answered testily. 'None of the swabs, the blood, vaginal and urine specimens have grown anything, apart from one throat swab. In two cases this has grown a fungus. It is not a fungus I know, and I have sent it off the Central Public Health Laboratory in London to have it identified.'

'It is very unusual to find a fungus as a primary source of infection,' interrupted Philip Boulton. 'Are you sure it's not a contaminant?'

There was a short silence, then Archie turned towards Philip and stared. 'Are you accusing me of running… an unhygienic laboratory?'

He stretched out the last two words so his listeners

were left in no doubt that if he was accused of running a brothel in one of the seedier parts of Medenby it would be considered marginally less offensive.

'No need to be bothered, Archie,' Philip added gaily. 'After all, Alexander Fleming discovered penicillin through contamination.'

Archie was not impressed. 'I knew Alexander Fleming; he was a great researcher, but not a brilliant administrator, and my lab has always been ten times cleaner than his ever was – and, in any case, he discovered penicillin by mistake.' Archibald Patterson was not a generous man, and even though Fleming was a fellow Scot, it was not enough to gain his approval.

James had to take control again. 'So it is reasonable to conclude that, at present, there is no reason to believe that the Poleaxe Syndrome is caused by a known bacterium. But, could it be caused by a virus or another infectious agent?'

Archie remained on his feet. He was not going to yield his important place at this meeting. 'Yes, that is possible. We canna detect viruses in our laboratory. But what I can say is that a straightforward bacterial infection can, and should be, excluded. If a bacterium is the cause, it is one we have never seen before.'

After saying these words firmly and slowly, he sat down, as this mildly menacing statement showed he was still a player in the diagnostic chase.

'Thank you, Dr Patterson, for a well-rounded statement.' James wanted to be accurate, even though he felt the summary would have been better if somewhat less well-rounded. He now turned to Philip. 'Can you help us here? What can the blood tests tell us?'

Philip Boulton considered most topics in life to be mildly amusing, and the Poleaxe Syndrome was no exception. His view was that much medical drama was comedy underneath. 'Well, I've not that much to toss into the ring. But there is something curious you need to know. The erythrocyte sedimentation rate is a little high in several of the Poleaxe cases. This indicates that there is likely to be some inflammation in the system but do not tell us where it is or how caused. So, all I can say is there is a flare-up somewhere and giving us all something to think about, even if it is only a minor piece in the diagnostic jigsaw.'

Christopher Barclay had been observing the events closely. 'It seems to me, from the standpoint of a general physician, that this syndrome is quite alarming. It does not seem to play by the rules that we know well in infection and medicine generally. I think we must be very careful not to rush in and make hasty conclusions.'

James was satisfied all the hospital staff had had their say. 'I fully agree with you, Dr Barclay. But we need to act quickly because the cases are increasing so quickly. I would now like to ask Madeleine about the distribution of the Poleaxe cases that have been reported so far. This is likely to give us clues about the nature of this unpleasant beast.'

Madeleine stood up, a little nervously, but James knew that she would be well prepared. Her nervousness stimulated good preparation, so she would present the data well.

When she spoke she was firm and clear. 'Of the sixty people with Poleaxe reported to date, all had contact with the first seventeen cases, all of whom we have identified within a radius of two miles from the town centre. I would like to concentrate on these. There were three clusters: one of five in Central Park, another of four close to the restaurant in Hope Street near the town square and another of five by the public library. There were also three other cases in different parts of the town.'

'Any sex difference?' asked Charles.

'Seven men, ten women. All aged between eighteen and sixty-five. Only two of them, brother and sister, were related.'

'And what were they doing before they collapsed?' asked Philip. 'The health visitors in our department are continuing to investigate this, but at present there is no consistent pattern. The ones in the park were having a lunch break and had just had sandwiches bought from a shop in the High Street, the ones found by the restaurant may have been eating there but we are not certain, and we are still making enquiries about the library group.'

'We need to know more about the Poleaxe patients in Blocks G and H. How are they, Matron?' James needed everyone to have a say at this first meeting. He realised that ignoring those who had been specially invited could lead to potential for resentment.

Matron Arbuthnot was brisk and efficient. 'I've just come back from the ward. Everything is as settled as it could be under the circumstances. Five are still unconscious but the others have woken up. Most are confused and, to some extent, bemused by everything going on. I am also glad to say that our barrier nursing is successful and all the staff are well. We are trying to play down the increase in cases as something that we all expected.'

After more questions it was clear that not enough was yet known to make any useful conclusions, so James felt it was time to draw the meeting to a close. 'Thank you all again for coming. At this stage I hope I can get your agreement to continue the present policy of isolation and containment on the basis that this could well be a new infectious disease. Nothing has been said that contradicts this, and in view of the potential dangers of mass infection, the present strategy may be the safest one.'

William Fothergill intervened. *Typical*, thought James, *he always has to put his neb in at the end.*

'It is fair to add that nothing has been said that confirms an infection, either, but it is certainly reasonable to continue the present policy.'

'Excellent,' said James, rising to his feet to indicate the end of the meeting. 'Shall we meet again at the same time next week, when we should have a great deal more information to digest?'

As he returned to his car in the April sunshine, James felt very satisfied with the work of the morning. He had chaired the meeting well, he had prevented alarm, public health in Medenby was now more respected, and he, as its head, was beginning to be appreciated as a valuable part of the medical establishment.

SIX

DAY FOURTEEN, SIXTY-THREE CASES, FIVE DEATHS

While the individual man is an insoluble puzzle, in the aggregate he becomes a mathematical certainty

Arthur Conan Doyle, 1890

'Are we all here now?' asked James, somewhat unnecessarily, as he knew the team was all there, but it was his standard way of getting started.

The chattering stopped in the small briefing room. The cups of coffee stopped clinking.

'This is an important meeting to update us all, as we have a suspicion Poleaxe is getting out of control and drastic action may be needed. I want to go back to the initial cases, as the clues to the cause must be found there. I think Madeleine has some very useful feedback.'

Madeleine cleared her throat. 'We have established the most likely place where Poleaxe started in Medenby but still do not know how it is being transmitted. All five of the initial cases had one common historical feature. They were in Central Park between the hours of 11am and 3pm on Monday 3rd April. I have prepared a map of the park with the help of my three colleagues and have added a rough idea of the times the five people came into the park.'

She pinned a primitive drawing of Central Park and its entrances on an easel. Madeleine continued. She was now well into the details and wanted to be as precise as possible.

'Before they came to the park, the five behaved very differently. Two of them bought sandwiches from the booth at the entrance and were eating them there. But there were only two who ate sandwiches. We have checked the ingredients in other sandwiches from the same source and found no pathogens in them. So I think we can safely exclude botulism, typhoid, E. coli and other food-transmitted diseases, especially as the other three were not exposed. But, despite this, all five experienced the Poleaxe symptoms within around four hours of being in the park.'

She looked again at her notes.

'This where we get into unknown territory. I have made this extra map of where each of the five went after being in the park.'

She pinned another map of the park, with lines showing the most likely movements of the five people. It looked like a London Underground map; each person was shown in lines of different colour.

'This shows how each of the five came into, and then left, the park. If they happened to be infectious then, assuming this is an infection, this may be useful later. As for the origin of Poleaxe, this is still far from clear.'

Madeleine had run out of words, so she sat down. James was impressed by her industry and achievements in such a short time. But although she presented her contribution well, he knew she needed reinforcement. Her self-confidence was eggshell-thick; it needed very little pressure to crack. She was also fiercely loyal to James. He was likely to need this in the future.

'Well done, Madeleine, you've expressed that very, very well. We're getting the picture forming now. Can you add anything more from your enquiries, Giles?'

Giles was keen to join in. He was enthusiastic about his role as detective and had found valuable clues.

'I have a suspicion that the key person we need to understand is Julia Unwincroft. She was showing symptoms before the others and was clearly unwell when she sat down in the park. It is not exactly clear, because some of their recollections were vague, but it looks as though all the other four were aware of this and tried to look after her, but I will need to check with Madeleine later. The other important bit of information is that Julia arrived from Singapore only a few hours earlier.'

James's attention focused on this immediately. This was turning out to be public health enquiry at its best.

'And why is that important?'

'All the others who have developed Poleaxe so far either come from Medenby or have been visiting the town from nearby. If we assume that Poleaxe is alien to Medenby, and probably England as a whole – and I agree, this is only an assumption – then it has probably been introduced from outside.'

'So you think Julia Unwincroft is the source?'

'I can't be certain of this, but the way I look at this is for her to be regarded as the source until we have other evidence.'

'Have you any suggestions to make about the nature of the disease?'

'Well, here's my first stab at it, James. But don't quote me on this, as I only found about the possibility last night when looking at a textbook of neurology. I'm studying for my medical membership now and was revising. There is an unusual form of encephalitis found in the Far East, Japanese encephalitis, that leads to symptoms very similar to Poleaxe. I could persuade myself that the clinical presentation of Julia Unwincroft when I first examined her was that of Japanese encephalitis.'

'That's an absolutely fascinating lead. Have you told the other physicians yet?'

'No. As I said, I only found out about this last night.'

'I'll get in touch with Dr Fothergill immediately after this meeting and let him know.'

James was pleased that neither Giles nor Madeleine had disclosed their findings. He would be the first to inform the hospital staff. It would show them that public health had a key role in the Poleaxe enquiry and would properly be in the vanguard of discovery.

The phone rang. It was Matron Arbuthnot. 'Dr Portown, I'm sorry to report that we have just had five new cases admitted, all looking like the Poleaxe Syndrome.'

'Thank you, Matron. I am with my team now and we'll get up to speed on this immediately.'

He turned towards the others. Tension was rising in the room. James was ready to give orders. Staccato, crisp and clear.

'You probably heard that. Five more cases. We may have an epidemic on our hands, even a pandemic. Giles, could you get straight back to the hospital and find out as much as possible about these new cases? Where they had been and who were possible contacts. Madeleine and Amanda, go now and make six copies of the map, with all the dates added, and give four to Giles to take with him. Can we meet again here in four hours to review and recap?'

They all rose from their chairs simultaneously. James decided not to phone William, that laid-back epitome of smuggery. He would emphasise the impact of their discoveries by visiting the Fothergill wolf in his lair. Public health was leading the charge; general medicine was dawdling in the ranks.

SEVEN

DAY SEVENTEEN, SEVENTY-FOUR CASES, FIVE DEATHS

In every mess I find a friend
Charles Dibdin, 1795

Barbara was now better again. What had happened a few days ago was utterly mysterious. She thought she had recovered from the dreaded Poleaxe but, clearly, whatever its origin, it was still inside her. She had lost control of her arms and legs again for no apparent reason and at first could not move them at all.

But, after she had been lifted up and carried back to her bed again, she had recovered their use completely within a couple of hours. She found it hard to believe, and continued to test out her arm muscles and repeat her straight leg raising, but the physiotherapist had told her not to bother, as she now had full function again. But she had been advised to walk around the ward with a Zimmer frame in case she suddenly lost control again.

So she was up and out again this morning as though nothing had happened. She was also able to meet the other four patients who had all been admitted with Poleaxe at the beginning of the epidemic. They had, unoriginally but predictably, been christened the 'Famous Five' by the nurses and enjoyed a status in the ward not shown to the others. They also gave encouragement to the staff and other patients, as they all, except one of them, were improving, unlike many of those who had been admitted later, four of whom had died. But all the more recent cases had gone to Block H and the patients in Block G had not been told.

Barbara first went to see Fred Entwistle, the only one who was not showing much improvement. She manoeuvred her way around to his bed and leant over him.

'Good morning, Fred. Yet another one for you to enjoy.'

'And all the better for being started off by you. You're my lady of the lamp, lighting up my day. I wish yer could wake me up every morning.'

Barbara sat down beside him and squeezed his hand. 'You give me a lift too, Fred. I find it hard to feel normal here, but seeing you helps a lot. But how are you now? Have you got the feeling back in your arms and legs?'

'Not exactly. I can hardly move them. But it doesn't help having all these bruises. They're giving me no end of pain.'

'What exactly happened when you got this Poleaxe?'

'I was right up in the top of Medenby Parish Church. I was ringing the bells. It always bothers me going up there, as I've got this nervous disposition, like. Yer know, claustrophobia, I think they call it. Feeling all het up in

44

a confined space. Don't feel I can get out, so I panic. But they're very short of bell-ringers, and so I had to help them out, and I were trained in Bolton where I grew up fifty years ago. Once you learn to bell-ring, yer never forget it.' Fred turned towards Barbara and smiled; he tried to lever himself up on his elbows but failed.

'Yes, I know about bell-ringing. My dad's a Methodist minister and I've learnt a bit, but never stuck at it.'

'Well, my oh my. Another bell-ringer. We're a dying breed, yer know. We need more young 'uns like you to carry us forward. As yer know something about it, I'll tell you exactly what happened. We were playing this quarter peal – quite complicated, as yer might know – and I were pulling hard on the sally – the fat bit of the rope – and, in the blinking of an eye, my arms and legs went dead. Of course the rope then went all over the place. But that was the last thing I remember – that is, until I came round in hospital.

'But that were only the start of it. There I was, like a sack of potatoes, like, at the top of this tower. The spiral staircase up to the tower is very narrow. So the only way they could get be down was to put me in a long bag, with one bell-ringer at one end and t'other at t'other end, and tek me down the steps. But it must have been a struggle, as when I came round in hospital I had all these bruises where they'd knocked me against the sides of a tower. I looked like a punch bag, and feel like I've bin stuck all over with pins. But nowt was broken, so I've reason to be thankful.'

Barbara was impressed. 'That's a story and a half. You make me feel as though I ought to be bell-ringing again. I could fill in the gap.'

'If yer could, that would be champion. They'll love to have you. And it's dead easy when yer've done it before.'

Barbara squeezed his hand again. He had livened up and looked better after telling his story. She must talk to him again. 'I want to hear more of your stories, happier ones next time. But I'm off to see the others now. They're all up and about. Hope you are too soon.'

She left his bed, clicking her Zimmer frame on the floor as she made her way to the dayroom. She entered just as a dark shower cloud suddenly clothed the previously bright blue sky and rain spattered the windows.

Like Poleaxe, Barbara thought, *just after it brightens up, it gets dark again.*

The three other members of the Famous Five were sitting together: Julia Unwincroft, Mary Beckinsale and Henry Carpenter. They had left their Zimmer frames by the entrance and were chatting over tea. Barbara joined them at the table, pleased to grasp a reminder of pre-Poleaxe days. Patterns of existence that were familiar now had great meaning. It was even better that everybody had their masks off, as although this was not officially allowed, it had become clear that Poleaxe cases could not reinfect themselves, and so some latitude was allowed.

They were all discussing their experiences before Poleaxe had hit them. Mary was talking. 'It's all a bit of a blur, really. You see, I've got this condition – agro-something, they call it – so I'm like a jelly when I'm on my own out of doors. But I live on my own with my books for company, and I had to go to the library to renew my card. So I was walking through the park to the bus station, getting all het up 'cos I can't stand those open spaces as they always bring

46

on a panic. Then, boom, that was it. Curtains for me until I came round here.'

'I was in the park too, and I'm a bit on the nervous side, so I think we've got something in common.' It relieved Barbara to admit this; she felt she was among friends.

'Mine's got similar connections,' said Julia. 'I'd just come back from Singapore, and after a long flight and train journey I was quite exhausted. Travel really gets me worked up and takes it out of me, because I'm always expecting something terrible to happen. So, while waiting for my friend Jean to pick me up, I was resting in the park. I must have gone to sleep. I remember walking about in a daze and then everything seemed to stop until I woke up here.'

'We are birds of a feather,' said Henry, whose face Barbara noted to be twitching a little. 'I'm nervous too, and even walking into town turns on my worry machine. But there was no choice. I had to come as I had an appointment with the employment people. I'm too frightened to go on buses, so I walked all the way from Ollington and had to stop in the park and have a sandwich to recover. Then everything seemed to go round in circles until I turned up here.'

The four of them looked at each other in silence and sipped their tea, munching the dry NHS biscuits, which Barbara surreptitiously dunked in her cup when she thought nobody was looking. They silently contemplated the May shower as it passed overhead and was replaced by bright sunshine.

Barbara felt unreasonably contented. She was in a hospital, had a condition nobody could understand and which might be very serious indeed, and was surrounded by strangers. She did not have Fred's claustrophobia, Mary's agoraphobia, Theresa's travel worries or Henry's fear of bus travel, but could appreciate all their symptoms well. She herself was normally nervous and self-conscious in company and had experienced all these symptoms, but as all the others had too, there was no inhibition in expressing them.

It did not help that in her everyday life so many people seemed to be looking at her. Often she was reminded by her friends that this was just a natural consequence of being attractive. No matter how little make-up she used and how tousled her hair was, she could not avoid being noticed.

'Let's face it, Barbara,' her best friend Amy had said, 'you're a head-turner. You may not like it, but lots of us would love to be in your position.'

But that was no help.

'If your face shone like a beacon and your lips trembled every time you were looked at, Amy, you wouldn't be so happy.'

To Barbara, being a head-turner was a head-churner. There was the world outside, full of excitement and opportunity, but once exposed to the unwanted attention of others, she was forced back into her personal prison of self-consciousness and rumination. This was why she craved the anonymity of crowds. She suspected people like Amy could never appreciate her suffering, as her defences were so well prepared. Anxiety was just a word to her, not a lifetime affliction.

Yet here, in this curious, alien environment, she was just another patient whom the nurses looked after well and wished back to good health, and people like Fred,

Julia, Henry and Mary did not pry into her affairs, talked naturally and looked at her normally. She already felt a bond with them; perhaps it was a consequence of shared adversity.

But there was another aspect that puzzled her. All the Famous Five were constitutionally nervous, or at least seemed to be. Was this a consequence of Poleaxe or were they all like this beforehand? And was the reason she felt so comfortable the shared bond of being anxious together, and not afraid to admit it? These were interesting questions that she must explore further. As a student of anthropology, she found other people endlessly fascinating, and here in the ward there were many opportunities to study.

Barbara climbed back into bed and continued thinking. Poleaxe was a mystery, but although it was frightening, it was not completely terrible. She hoped the doctors would sort it out in time, but she might be able to help them understand it better. Of course, she was only a student at the beginning of intellectual discovery, but already she had some knowledge in place. Poleaxe struck without warning; it affected her muscles, but not her thinking; it came and went at different times; and it seemed to pick out people who were constitutionally nervous.

That was not a bad start, and she was proud of herself for knitting these different points together. And despite being in a confined environment, excluded from the open air and surrounded by illness, here she was beginning to feel free. Nobody expected anything from her, she was able to meet interesting people and she was giving pleasure to all, quite effortlessly, just by being herself. This was a new experience that she relished, so very different from life at home. She clearly had to work on these qualities that she only dimly knew she had. At nineteen, she had thought she was fully grown. There was a lot of developing ahead.

EIGHT

DAY TWENTY, NINETY-THREE CASES, SIX DEATHS

*Examinations are formidable even to the best prepared, for
the greatest fool may ask more than the wisest man can answer*

Charles Colton, 1820

Barbara woke up from a daze to see a handsome man in a white coat looking at her.

'I am Dr Charles Merridew. I'm a neurologist, and you must be Barbara Dukinfield.'

Barbara nodded but did not answer, as she was too busy trying to quench the fires in her face. She could only hope this Dr Kildare figure would not be sticking needles into her. Most of the others who came to see her did exactly that but did not give a proper explanation of what they were doing.

'I've come to see you, as you're a conundrum.'

She liked the thought of being a conundrum. It was better than just being a patient.

'What I want to do is to give you a full neurological examination, as it might help me to understand this Poleaxe Syndrome a little better.'

Barbara was now getting confident enough to engage with strange people who came to see her and her face had now returned to its normal colour. 'I don't want to appear rude, but it would be very helpful if you could explain what you are doing in your examination, as I would like to know what is going on.'

Charles blinked. 'Of course. I quite understand. I would feel exactly the same if I was in your position and wasn't a neurologist. Anyway, it will keep me on my toes.'

This was a good start. Barbara would make the most of the opportunity. Charles drew the curtains round her bed and approached from her right side. He pulled the bedclothes back and looked at her closely.

'Can I ask what you are doing just at the moment?'

'I am checking your appearance, whether the right and left sides of your body are equal and symmetrical, whether your face is also symmetrical, and whether you have any abnormal movement in your arms and legs. As you know only too well, this Poleaxe goes for the limbs. But I can see nothing untoward here. I am now going to check your reflexes with this object.'

He pulled out a plastic rod, one end pointed and the other with a round black rubber disc, from his bag.

'This is called a patellar hammer, but it's not a hammer at all, just hard rubber that allows me to check the reflexes in your nerves and muscles.'

He tapped with the hammer just below the left kneecap before quickly doing the same with the right.

Each of Barbara's legs below the knee jumped upwards a few inches.

'What does that tell you?'

'That your knee reflexes are normal. By tapping on the tendon attached to the muscle I set up a circuit to the nerves in your back that tells your muscles to contract and so raises the leg. That shows me that the nerve circuits in your leg are intact and working well.'

He carried out a similar test by tapping the big tendon above her ankles. There was a smaller jump upwards.

'Good, that's normal too.'

He then turned the hammer round and, with the pointed end, stroked the side of her left heel down to the little toe. He did the same with the right heel. Both of Barbara's big toes went down.

'Is that a different test, not just checking if I'm ticklish, 'cos I am?'

'Yes. The other tests were checking the outer, or peripheral, nerves. This test checks if the inner nerves, up in the brain area, are all working properly. If they are not, the big toe goes up.'

He continued his examination, methodically and carefully. He looked into the back of her eyes with a torch-like device called an ophthalmoscope, into her ears with a similar instrument and at the back of her throat too. He tested her voice, her ability to see objects at the edge of her vision when looking straight ahead – he said he was testing her visual fields – and finished by idly putting the sharp end of the patellar hammer above and below her belly button.

'Good, abdominal reflexes working very well too.'

'So, can I ask for your conclusions, Dr Merridew? Am I, as you might say, neurologically intact, and am I still a conundrum?'

'You are an inquisitive young lady, aren't you? But you may still be a conundrum, as I do not have any clear answers. I am more or less satisfied that there are no after-effects of Poleaxe on your body, but still am not sure what has gone on in your nervous system and would like to recommend one further test.'

'Not another blood test, I hope?'

'No, it is a special test to measure your brain waves. It is called an electroencephalogram.'

Barbara felt a surge of panic. This sounded terrifying. 'You mean you're going to get inside my brain and find out all that commotion inside. Do I have to have this test? Does it involve an operation?'

'No, young lady. Do not be alarmed. The test only records your brain waves from electrodes on the surface of your head. It is not invasive and is also quite painless, if a trifle boring. But thank you for all your questions. They have helped me enormously, as sometimes medical students cannot follow what I am saying, and I realise now how I must go about explaining what is still a very complicated subject.'

He made as to move away, but Barbara had an idea. 'Could you just test that heel reflex again?'

'Of course.'

He repeated the test and Barbara's toes went up.

'I must have tickled you this time. The test isn't always reliable. I hope to see you again after all the tests have been completed.'

Barbara lay back as Charles drew the curtains again and left. She could see Giles in the corner of the ward and attracted his attention. She was feeling relaxed again now, and Giles was always reassuring in what still felt like an alien place much of the time.

'I see you have been seeing the great Dr Merridew. We call him the brain of Medenby. He knows everything and then a little more – it's so infuriating. What's he been doing?'

'He's given me a full neurological examination. But can I ask you to get a patellar hammer for me?'

'Of course, there's always several on the ward.'

He returned a few seconds later.

'Could you just test my heel reflex again? I think you know how to do it.'

Giles duly did so. Barbara's toes went down.

'Yes, that's quite normal. Did Dr Merridew find the same?'

'Yes, he did, but only the first time he tested me. Later on he told me I had to have one of those brain wave tests – electroenceff something – and it sounded so awful I nearly had a full blown panic attack. So just to be certain, I asked him to test me again, and this time my toes went up.'

'Are you absolutely sure about that, Barbara?'

'Of course I am. Dr Merridew noticed it too and said he must have tickled me first and I just moved my toes away, so it wasn't a reflex. But I know it was. I couldn't control my toes; they just went up. And I think I know why.'

'You are getting very mysterious, Barbara, but I've got an idea what you are going to say.'

'Of course you have, Giles. My nervous system is all right more most of the time, but when I get very anxious it goes haywire, but only temporarily, until I get back on an even keel. It's funny how people with anxiety complain about their nerves. In my case it's absolutely right. My anxiety can foul up my nervous system, not just figuratively or by analogy, but directly. The change must have been caused by Poleaxe.'

'I really think you're right, Barbara. I must tell the others about this. We're beginning to find the answers now.'

Barbara sat back, feeling very satisfied. She wondered what the brain wave test would show. She wanted it to say, 'Barbara Dukinfield is right; please listen to her, forget these silly tests.'

NINE

DAY TWENTY-TWO, ONE HUNDRED AND ONE CASES, EIGHT DEATHS

But I will be a bridegroom in my death

William Shakespeare, *Antony and Cleopatra, 1623*

Fred Entwistle was not getting better, but nobody could understand why. His bruises were healing, he was in much less pain, but his arms and legs were still useless, and he was beginning to despair. Barbara, with her constant need to be of help to everybody, had to do what she could. And he never appeared to be getting other visitors.

She sat down next to Fred. His face was grey and drawn, but he forced a wan smile.

'Here's my lady of the lamp again.'

'But I haven't got a lamp, Fred.'

'Course you have. It's in yer face and yer smile. But I think my own lamp will be going out soon, lass.'

'Don't be ridiculous, Fred, it's just that, you being older, recovery takes more time.'

Barbara recognised she was talking in her schoolmarmy voice, but it was right for the occasion and she couldn't stop it. And she must work hard to get Fred out of this bad spot.

'No, I'm not into melodrama, but I've 'ad a good innings, and I think my time has come. Yer know, as I've got older, life's got more of a struggle, and I get so worked up over everything now. I'm lying in this bed, not able to move, going over an' over again all the things that have happened in my life and where I've gone wrong.'

'But it can't be all bad. Come on, now. Tell me some of the things you've been proud of.'

'I'll have to scratch all round my brain to find anything.' He paused. 'I've found summat, but it goes back a long way. When I were at school in Farnworth, near where I was born, now that is a long time ago, there was a teacher who took a proper interest in my education. He picked up that I was good at mathematics… ee no, yer won't want to know about this.'

'I do want to know, Fred. Please go on.'

'Well, Barbara, this teacher, Herbert Taylor, was very good, but he wasn't the greatest at keeping order in the class. And for some reason the other kids decided to give him a silly nickname, Big Nose. That were funny, 'cos he didn't have a big nose at all. But once it caught on everyone started using it. And of course he knew all about it, and I could see it really bothered him. People who knew about it said he was going to give up teaching.'

'That would have been terrible.'

'That's what I thought. So one time, when he got called out of class and everybody started shouting "Big Nose" at the tops of their voices, I stood up, went to the front of the class and shouted, "I want you lot all to shut up. He hasn't got a big nose, he hasn't even got a small nose, but what I do know is that he's a bloody good teacher and you've got to stick with him." And you know what happened? They all shut up; I think I must have shamed them. Afterwards it all stopped and it were though it 'ad never happened.'

'So you were justly proud of that. And I'm proud to hear you tell it to me.'

'It mattered to me because he got me through my exams so I could become a draughtsman. It really set me up for my working life.'

Barbara wanted more of this. It would really cheer him up. 'That's a lovely story. And I'm sure that there are many more episodes in Fred Entwistle's life that are worth reporting. But I have noticed, Fred, that you have had no visitors while you have been here. Have you any family?'

'Nowt. I never married. Nervous type that I am, had enough trouble looking after misself, never wanted the extra responsibility. Of course, I had the odd fling, but who hasn't?'

'So you live on your own, then?'

'Yes, in one of those little old houses in Albert Street. It's small, but it does champion.'

'Well, I'm going to visit you there when you come out of hospital. So you had better hurry up and get better.'

Barbara recognised that this urge to help everybody, mercifully exploited by her mother, was not always wise, but on this occasion, she knew it was absolutely right.

'Yes, that would be nice. But it's not likely that I'll be going home soon. I'm just a nervous wreck now, ready for the knacker's yard. It's when you feel really restless and can't move, that's when it gets to you. I bet to you I'm looking quite calm lying here, but I'm proper seething inside. Oh no, the clappers are going again.'

'What do you mean, Fred?'

'It's my ticker. It's banging away in my chest, louder and louder. When it gets to its full level I think I'll burst.'

It was odd. Fred had not moved, but the blood had drained out of his face and he looked as though he was in agony.

'No, no, Fred. You're just having a panic attack. A panic attack never killed anybody. You'll settle down soon.'

But Barbara was getting bothered. Fred was looking awful. His face was quivering, his eyes were going glassy and he really couldn't get his breath.

'I think I'm going, lass. Could you just hold my hand? I'd like you to be with me.'

Barbara complied. There was not much else she could do. 'Now just rest quietly, Fred, and let this pass over you.'

Fred stopped talking and appeared to be resting quietly again. Barbara continued to hold his hand. What else could she do? But after a little while, he was no longer squeezing hers. She looked at him closely. He wasn't moving, but he did not seem to be sleeping. He just lay there. She passed a hand over his face.

Then she guessed correctly.

'Nurse,' she shouted at the top of her voice. 'We need some help.'

Before the nurse came, she put her head in her hands and quietly wept.

TEN

DAY THIRTY, ONE HUNDRED AND FOUR CASES, NINE DEATHS

There is nothing in the world so irresistibly contagious as laughter and good humour

Charles Dickens, 1843

Block G was now a trifle happier. The number of new cases had fallen a little, the peak may have been reached, but people were still dying. Matron Arbuthnot felt it necessary to give pep talks to the patients under her care and these were steadily becoming more optimistic. 'Now I know some of you were feeling mis a few days ago. But the news is now good. They know what causes this Poleaxe Syndrome now and we're well on the way to beating it.' This was not true, but she had learnt that exaggerated optimism was a great enabler of health.

Barbara was still worried that people were dying. How could some of the nurses shrug this off, especially when some of them had succumbed? She could not stop thinking about Fred's death. He had disappeared off the planet and after a few words of commiseration he had been forgotten – totally. Of course, on reflection this was understandable. Nurses were used to death; it came with their territory, and Poleaxe was still a battlefield with lots of casualties.

It was good that visiting time was starting; it prevented rumination. Barbara was a people-watcher. Being in a hospital bed was not a handicap when you could sit with impunity and look at all the overdressed visitors with their fussy hats, gushing greetings, bunches of flowers and little presents for the bedridden patients. Some of the presents were quite inappropriate for people with Poleaxe. So jigsaws, puzzles, crossword books and knitting patterns were left unopened by the beds of those who were only just beginning to get feeling and movement back into their arms and fingers. But no matter what was brought, the visits were always welcome, and Barbara loved to see the faces light up as each visitor was recognised and entered into full consciousness.

But what was this? Someone was standing beside her bed.

'Glad to be able to see you again, even if last time we were anonymous.'

Barbara liked the voice, firm but with a tickle of humour, and was sure she had heard it before. Yes, the shiny brown shoes were the clue. The strange man who occupied them was also shiny and interesting. Round-faced, merry and with a chunky frame. But who exactly was he?

'Sorry to leave you looking puzzled. I'm Danny Preston. I came to see you by mistake a few weeks ago. No,

I'm confusing you even more. I was visiting my sister but got the wrong bed at first, so we had a funny conversation through the curtains.'

'Of course. I remember you said your name was Danny. And you gave me a book by mistake. *Catch-22*, now that was an eye-opener. Couldn't make up my mind if it was anti-war, anti-authority or just plain crazy, but it was a thundering good read.'

'Yes, I couldn't help thinking about the book too. I thought I was in a catch-22 situation too. I wanted to see you again, but as I had never seen you, I would not recognise you. But if you saw me you would not be able to recognise me either. So if you had left the hospital and I had asked to see you here, they would never have told me anything, as I only knew your name.'

Barbara had read the book, more than once, as it had been her main reading matter for some days. 'Yes, but you hadn't finished. For you to want to see Barbara Dukinfield, without knowing who she was, is a sign of complete insanity. But the fact you made the effort to puzzle out where Barbara might be, and showed up, suggested you might be sane. That is the catch-22. Now I have to decide whether you are sane or insane.'

Danny hooted with admiration. 'You certainly have been an industrious reader. But what is your verdict? Am I sane or insane?'

'I am far from sure. I am studying anthropology at university and have been taught not to make my mind up too quickly when faced with strange people.'

Danny was enjoying this repartee. She could see his eyes twinkling. 'In that case, I will have to come and see you again, and when I am slightly less strange you can tell me your decision.'

Barbara screwed up her face and thought. 'Yes, I think I would like that, but if you are a complex character it may take some time, and at present I am not able to give you a certificate of sanity.'

Danny hooted again.

'But I would like to be a little more serious. I seem to remember that the time you came before, you were visiting your sister. But I am not sure if I have seen her on the ward.'

Danny also reverted to seriousness. 'No. They thought my sister Jane had Poleaxe to begin with but then they realised it wasn't, so they moved her out of this ward. She's now been diagnosed with multiple sclerosis. It's a nervous system disorder. The doctors think she has a less serious form of the condition and now she's much better. The problem is that nobody can predict relapses in this condition.'

The two continued chatting, easily and happily, despite the curious circumstances of the visit and the unusual setting. Barbara could not help sharing her worries that Poleaxe may be just like multiple sclerosis. Although she was better now, there was no guarantee that the paralysis would not recur. She also could not help mentioning to Danny her funny notion that anxiety might have something to do with Poleaxe, as all the people she had spoken to with the condition seemed to be excessively nervous.

'And I have to admit that I'm in the same category too. I'm a very nervous person. I see troubles round the corners nobody else has seen as they are so far away. But I would like to think it's because the effects of my upbringing are lasting longer than they should.'

It was time for Danny to go. 'I'm off to see Jane now. But remember, I definitely need to see you again as you have to pronounce on my sanity, a very important subject dear to my heart.'

'Of course, the anthropologist is always here, but remember, she is not a psychiatrist. She studies peoples only. She can only guess when it comes to individuals.'

'I'll take a chance on that. That means, whatever your verdict, I can share it with all those other Dannys I know who are exactly like me.'

Barbara watched as Danny strode confidently out of the ward. She had certainly been enthused, but was she also excited? Perhaps it was just the sound of the Beatles singing 'All My Loving' in the ward background, but she could not be sure.

But one thing she was sure about after her amusing interlude. She must let others know about her Poleaxe anxiety theory. Perhaps it was now approaching a fact. It was odd that so alarming a threat could be so fascinating a companion. It was an odd story, but well worth telling.

ELEVEN

DAY THIRTY-THREE, ONE HUNDRED AND TWENTY CASES, TEN DEATHS

*Those comfortably padded lunatic asylums which are known
euphemistically as the stately homes of England*

Virginia Woolf, 1941

Stephen Bollider was taking his early-morning stroll. There
were only a few people walking up the hill to Middleshire
Hospital. The warnings about Poleaxe had made people
wary of going out in crowded places, but at this hour in the
morning it was bound to be safe and the dogs needed to be
walked. The grass glistened with dew, the air was still, and
as Stephen and the walkers looked up, they could see the
walls of Middleshire Hospital lit up in the April morning
sun, making it look a more friendly place than was implied
by its reputation.

Of course, everyone knew that the hospital was
still the nuthouse, more shortly expressed as 'the bin'.
Middleshire Hospital was the new name that had been

given to what all the older people in the town knew to be Medenby Borough Asylum. A new name air-brushing the old would not remove the stigma from the place built eighty years before. It had to be constructed within the bounds of the town so could not be like many other asylums. 'Out of sight, out of mind' was the national policy for these institutions in the Victorian era, but Medenby Hospital was a place not only in sight, but an incite for stigma. Stephen was aware of this stigma when he was appointed, and all its handicaps, when he first got appointed as a junior registrar. But as the hospital had a go-ahead medical director who was determined to develop mental health services in the community, he felt he was in the right place.

He had already settled into the job quickly. Although at first some of the staff regarded him as a bit of an egghead, accentuated by his waspish criticism of shoddy science and intolerance of dogma, he was respected for his energy and commitment. His colleagues all had the feeling he would go far, but were not sure in what direction.

He walked back past the lawn in front of the main building. The tulips in the lawn's solitary flowerbed were beginning to break through and spring was in the air and in his step. Everything suggested to Stephen that this was going to be a good day. He was pleased that Poleaxe, whatever its cause, was not having an impact on him or the hospital so it could be put to the back of his mind.

In any case, he had an important meeting this morning. The medical director had asked to see him. As Stephen was generally an optimist, he was convinced in advance that this would be a positive meeting, one that might promote his career. He strode into the headquarters building and knocked on the door marked 'Physician Superintendent'.

'Come in,' a voice said cheerily.

Stephen opened the door and walked gingerly over the cherry-red carpet to the desk. He had not been in this room before. It was right at the back of the headquarters building at the hospital, and though Stephen had often seen his boss, Dr David Wattis, at ward reviews, he never been in the office before. Like most of the buildings in the county asylum, the headquarters were reassuringly Victorian, solid and determined, built at a time when a surge of patients requiring mental health care needed to be accommodated by a beneficent society. But beneficence must not be unlicensed; it had to be tailored. Although the mentally ill needed to be cared for, they should be kept away from normal society. So there was another reason why the mental hospitals were out of sight. Their well-designed and functional buildings, erected in the countryside, were far away from other residential populations. But this had other advantages. Many of the mentally ill people had come from overcrowded slums that had sprung up after the Industrial Revolution. These people needed fresh air and space, and so each new asylum had acres of gardens where the residents could not only learn the skills of working on the land but also benefit the asylum by growing all their own fruits and vegetables. Most of them would be staying there for life, so it was important to make their living conditions as amenable as possible.

Stephen had been reminded of this ever since he had been working at the asylum. He and his wife, Pauline, had no home of their own but, like most junior doctors, had been offered accommodation in the asylum as part of the incentive for the position. After all, psychiatry was one of the least attractive parts of medicine and encouragement was needed for recruitment. So Stephen and Pauline were staying in a large and roomy flat with unnecessarily high ceilings and somewhat primitive cooking facilities but this was made up for by looking through the large sash windows to the fine hills beyond. But they were shortly going to move to a small terraced house in the town.

'Houses are cheap now,' his father, an insurance broker, had advised. 'This is the time to get on the ladder.'

Stephen looked around as he waited for Dr Wattis to finish examining some correspondence. A coal fire burnt merrily in the grate beside him. The setting would not have been out of place fifty years ago.

David Wattis looked up after completing a signature. 'Sorry to be so preoccupied, but I've just received a curious letter and I think you might be able to help.'

Stephen was intrigued.

'You may have heard about these cases of the Poleaxe Syndrome at Medenby. The conventional wisdom is that this is a serious infectious disease and this is why everyone is so alarmed about it. But two days ago, I received this letter' – he picked up a pale yellow sheet and waved it at Stephen – 'and I wanted to discuss with you.'

'What does it say?'

'I'm sorry, I cannot show it to you in full as it is very sensitive. In any case, it is anonymous, but the important words, written in capitals, are written on the other side.'

David turned the sheet over to show to Stephen, who read, 'MY VIEW IS THAT POLEAXE IS, AT LEAST PARTLY, A MENTAL DISEASE. PLEASE HELP.'

'This sounds very interesting,' said Stephen, now even more intrigued, 'but where does this involve me?'

'I'll be quite frank with you, but I am relying on your ability to keep this letter confidential. There have been rumours that the Poleaxe Syndrome is not what it seems and that the attempts to find an infectious agent are not moving forwards very fast. You are one of the best junior doctors in the asylum, sorry, our hospital, and I think you could act as our psychiatric detective. I know you go regularly to Medenby Hospital to see patients after they have harmed themselves and so you are already well known there. What I would like you to do is to find a good reason to go over to see some of the patients in block G where all the Poleaxe patients are and make your assessment. If any have got mental pathology, I'm sure you will be able to pick it up, and decide whether it is the main problem or only a secondary one.'

'But I never had reasons to go over to block G, and why do we have to be secret about it?'

'Stephen, the longer you are in psychiatry the more you will realise that we are still considered strange outsiders. Mental hospitals are places you go to under compulsion and escape from through accident. We are the black box of care; few know what we do and most prefer to remain in ignorance as long as we remain in our proper place. So moving into the community, and to general hospitals, where most people with mental illness happen to be, will be a hard struggle. So as far as Medenby is concerned, the medical view is that we should stay out of general hospital affairs. If we are to make an impact, I would like to be more confident before advertising our presence. As for going to Block G, I am sure I can rely on your ingenuity, Stephen. I am sure it is not beyond you to find someone who could invite you to assess one or more of the patients there. As you know only too well, most patients in hospital have some degree of mental distress, even though it is sadly often ignored, but when it is obvious, it is perfectly reasonable to ask for a psychiatric opinion.'

'You are investing a great deal of confidence in me, Dr Wattis. I cannot but admit that all this fascinates me, so I will do what I can and let you know. In any case, I agree with you. What is becoming known as liaison psychiatry is going to be the discipline of the future.'

TWELVE

DAY THIRTY-FOUR, ONE HUNDRED AND THIRTY-EIGHT CASES, TWELVE DEATHS

Before I built a wall I'd ask to know
What I was walling in or walling out,
And to whom I was like to give offence

Robert Frost, 1914

Lombard Street in Medenby was not at its best on this May morning. It was windy, and the steely drizzle that enveloped the town was a penetrating one. As Sir George Gribbins left his taxi, even the quick raising of an umbrella was not enough to prevent the rain from patterning his coat with shimmering tiny stars. As he walked he glanced at the signs above the doors along the street. There it was – Medenby Public Health Department. He knocked firmly on the door.

James opened the door nervously to see a large figure almost blotting out the light. He had the appearance of an avuncular farmer: tall but thickset, and with prematurely greying hair. He only had one eye and a monocle; the other eye seemed to be missing. James felt he would get on well with him; he was not one of the Fothergill types.

'I hope you had no problem in getting here, Sir George.'

'Not at all. The taxi took me straight from the station without any fuss. They seemed to expect me. You must have forewarned them.'

James nodded. They sat down as Amanda Smith provided coffee. She was a competent secretary but somewhat staid, and James worried that the Poleaxe saga might upset her equilibrium. But today she was secure in her own territory, pleased with the opportunity and preening herself that she, for the first time, was serving a knight of the realm.

Sir George picked up his coffee and looked round the room, turning his head slowly to take everything in. 'What I really need to know, James, is your thinking about the cause and implications of the Poleaxe Syndrome, especially from the national viewpoint. I know we are all in the dark, but you can see what is going on more than most. You can imagine it is creating quite a stir down in London, and ministers are asking me lots of questions.'

James liked it that he was addressed by his first name. This was a good start.

'How would you like me to proceed?'

'Just take me through it, chronologically, together with your thinking about it on the way. I'm in no rush.' Sir George settled back in his chair, pleased to be away from the tensions in Whitehall.

So James did as asked, as accurately as he could, but made it clear that all the evidence pointed towards an infective agent as the cause. The speed with which the disease had been transmitted, the course of the illness, the evidence of direct contact between those affected; it all pointed towards an infection. There was no other explanation.

Sir George picked this up quickly. So when James had finished, he honed in. 'So it is clear to me that you think an infectious agent was responsible for Poleaxe from the beginning. What made you so certain?'

'It was the epidemiology. Clusters of cases all appearing together, contact between all of them, dramatic increase in numbers over a few days; all this suggested an infective agent or some sort of poison. After exhaustive investigations, we feel poison can be completely ruled out, so we are left with infection.'

'But what about the negatives – no agent identified, no consistent blood or antibody changes, no evidence of form of transmission; don't they bother you?'

'Yes, but if, as I think, this is a completely new infective agent, I am not surprised we have made little progress here.'

'And now I really need your advice. What do you think we need to do now?' George's one eye and monocle were now fixed on James's face. He could almost feel it boring into his brain.

This was a crucial question for James, and one where he felt most vulnerable. But he had to follow his instincts here. And he felt he had a sympathetic audience. After all, Sir George was essentially a public health physician. He was bound to be on his side.

'We are in a very difficult position. Currently we are getting up to thirty new cases each day, almost all in the town, but including some who had travelled long distances from elsewhere were also getting infected – I mean affected, I suppose – and we had no idea how serious the illness was. As the disease is being transmitted so easily, I think at this point we need to seal the town off, lock down the town.'

Sir George was not convinced. 'But do you realise what disruption this will cause? It will create even more alarm and may make the problem so much worse in Medenby.'

'I am aware of that, Sir George. But just imagine if we had new cases in Nottingham, in Sheffield, in Lincoln or even further afield. All our evidence suggests that in large towns and cities, the rate of infection would increase astronomically.'

George sat back for a minute or too. He was clearly going to use his words carefully. 'I have to put to you a question, James. You are clearly convinced that Poleaxe is an infectious disease. I am inclined to agree with you. But let us consider some other possibilities. The cause may lie exclusively in the environment of Medenby. The water supply here may be contaminated by compounds of lead or those of other heavy metals that are highly poisonous. It may be that your food supply is similarly contaminated by a universal ingredient such as flour. Or it may be that the panic in Medenby – that I admit you are trying hard to control – is so serious that you have a psychological epidemic on your hands. In all these instances, sealing off the town may make matters worse.'

James pounced. 'I do not want to disagree with you, Sir George. Nobody could exclude other possibilities while we remain in the dark about this disease. But I do want to make it clear that I know the people of Medenby, and they would be on my side. They are not demonstrative people; they go about their daily business with little fuss and have a stoical quality in the face of adversity that is proving to be highly valuable in our dealings with them. They, in my view – and I think I can speak for them with some confidence – would be ready and willing to endure the difficulties and privations that would follow sealing off the town, and would be proud to be in the vanguard of our struggle to conquer this affliction.'

As he finished, he could not help thinking of the history of Medenby. After King John died in 1216, the country was close to anarchy and the invading French forces under Prince Louis were in danger of taking over. But Sir William Marshal, the most loyal knight of the realm, had mustered his forces in Medenby and marched to Lincoln where the French were routed and within a few months had been totally defeated. So Sir William's call to arms of 1216 was being re-enacted, albeit in a very different form.

Sir George was visibly impressed. Perhaps the strengths of Medenby had been underestimated. 'You have convinced me, James. I will authorise the quarantining of the town with my ministers and leave it to you and your colleagues to decide the points of entry and departure. I agree this is an urgent matter and hope it can be completed in the next few days. This disease is stealing time and we must catch up fast. Let us all hope you are right, and that we find the answer to it before too long.'

Sir George sighed. He had almost finished his enquiries. After clarifying the resources James needed to maintain public health services in the town he was ready to leave. But first he had a message for James.

'I appreciate the energy, enthusiasm and commitment you are making to understanding the Poleaxe Syndrome. It has certainly made you a national figure. It is also clear to me you have strong beliefs as to the cause. But strong beliefs are sometimes the enemy of reason, and I feel it only right to caution you a little. Please be open to new information as it transpires, weigh it up carefully, even if does not support your theory, and listen to the views of other experts.'

'Of course, I will, Sir George. You can rely on me to take your advice, and may I thank you for accommodating my concerns so carefully.'

Amanda organised the taxi back to the station. The rain had stopped and Sir George left as smoothly as he had arrived. The interview had gone well but still left James unsettled. 'Strong beliefs are the enemy of reason'. What exactly did he mean by this? Was he suggesting that James had gone too far, or not far enough? Did he think that the infection theory was oversold? And what about these other possibilities, especially the psychological one?

He stayed in the office to collect and organise all these thoughts. As he did on many similar occasions, he folded a sheet of paper longways and wrote 'GG' on the top, 'positives' on the left-hand side and 'negatives' on the right. When he had finished he was pleased to note that the positives had far exceeded the negatives. But the exercise had led to a clear task ahead. He wrote across the page at the bottom: 'INFECTION NEEDS TO BE UNEQUIVOCALLY PROVED.'

THIRTEEN

DAY FORTY-ONE, ONE HUNDRED AND FIFTY CASES, TWELVE DEATHS

Having had centuries of experience with the smallpox virus, the village elders had instituted their own methods for controlling the virus, according to their received wisdom, which was to cut their villages off from the world, to protect their people from a raging plague. It was reverse quarantine, an ancient practice in Africa, where a village bars itself from strangers during a time of disease, and drives away outsiders who appear

Richard Preston, 1994

The town of Medenby was adorned gloriously in the May sunshine as the police helicopter hovered overhead. It had rained overnight, and the rooftops and chimneys of the old houses sparkled and glistened, and these, lined with the streets running down towards the market square, gave the town the appearance of a giant corrugated whale basking before the challenges of the day. As the helicopter descended, it passed over the parish church and the old grey castle on the banks of the mighty River Brent, all adding to the impression of gentle and solid tranquillity. But further gaze showed that this conclusion was wrong. There were four new areas suggesting congestion and great activity. They were placed like the numbers on a clock face, roughly equidistant, and all on major roads going out of the town, each with a cluster of vehicles on either side.

Despite the apparent calm from the air, something approaching panic was being felt in Medenby. The number of cases had suddenly risen to 150, with more beginning to appear outside the town. There were also many people misdiagnosed. After an early-morning frost some people had slipped on ice and fallen. Poleaxe was automatically assumed to be the cause and, yet, once transferred to Medenby Hospital it was obvious they did not have the syndrome. So it became unwise to slip and to fall in the town; you would be observed from a distance but nothing would be done until the ambulances arrived.

It did not help that nobody had any idea of the cause. James had already anticipated the alarm that would arise from sealing off the town and had used his broadcasts on Radio Medenby accordingly.

'I know you, the people of Medenby. You are strong and determined, and do not give in. We are going to starve Poleaxe before beating it. We are close to finding the cause, but before we succeed, we must not allow it to come into contact with others. So what is the answer? It is simple. Knuckle down, and keep yourselves to yourselves.'

The next broadcast explained the reason for cutting off the town.

'We are now beginning to bring this disease under control. But we can only do this if we can stop people coming in and out of the town. So, with the agreement of the Department of Health, we are sealing off Medenby from the rest of the country. This is an emergency measure, but, I cannot emphasise too strongly, not a panic one. We will still be able to receive goods and other services from four crossing points that we will detail later on this programme. So much of life will go on as before. I only ask you to be patient. One of our famous poets, John Milton, wrote, "They also serve who only stand and wait". You too can serve by waiting and staying calm. And, people of Medenby, I know you can.'

The feedback was positive. Some people managed to get out of the town before the barriers went up, but the numbers were very small and a few were even returned by their relatives with cries of 'chicken' and 'cowards'. Medenby was prepared to knuckle down. It had survived three sieges in the Civil War; it could do so again.

The dramatic increase in the number of cases had now led to public health experts across the country believing that Poleaxe must have an infectious cause. There was general agreement that sealing off Medenby was entirely correct.

James explained this in more detail to his colleagues in the public health department. 'When there was the major outbreak of Spanish flu in 1918–20, it was clear that the cause was an infectious agent. In the case of Spanish flu, there was a massive death toll and only one place avoided it – Australia. They did this by imposing quarantine restrictions on all people entering the continent so that anybody that might be incubating the disease would not be mingling with the native population. What was the outcome? Complete freedom of Spanish flu from the continent of Australia. Medenby is the reverse of Australia, but it will make the rest of the country safe. We can now concentrate on finding the nature of the disease.'

So Medenby, quietly and without fuss, with excellent cooperation and coordination, was put into quarantine. All roads into the town were sealed off apart from the four principal roads into the town. Each of these had a checkpoint. Conveniently labelled, these were Checkpoint A for the Aslock Road to the south, Checkpoint B for the Beacon Road to the east, Checkpoint C for the Castle Road to the west and Checkpoint D for the Doncaster Road to the north. Goods could be transported across these checkpoints from the rest of the country to Medenby, but until the outbreak had been contained, this would not happen in the reverse direction. People were treated differently. They were not allowed to cross any of the checkpoints except in an emergency.

The helicopter landed close to Checkpoint C. James and Paddy Titton, the Head of Police in Medenby, climbed down. A small crowd at the barrier gave a smattering of applause. James was worried that they were not exactly following his advice about mixing together, but for some reason quite a few people had decided Poleaxe was going to miss them out. This was Medenby stubbornness at its best and worst, possibly unwise but still praiseworthy.

Paddy seemed pleased about the checkpoint operation. But he had some questions. 'Now we've done what we can, James. Are we going to beat Poleaxe now?'

'I am confident we can. As I have been saying in my broadcasts, we just want people to be both careful and calm. You and your force have been tremendous in moving so smoothly in segregating the town. We just have to sit back, hope and pray that new cases fall steadily, and that our lab boys can find the cause of the disease. But I have confidence in the people of this town. Some people feel they lack spirit or give in too easily, but I know them better. They stick at tasks, they look ahead, they face danger and do not surrender to alarm. I do not know what we bred out of them in the Civil War, but we now have a people of stout purpose who are our main asset in the fight.'

'I'm pleased you can say that,' added Paddy. 'Our force is right behind you. We must stick at this together.'

FOURTEEN

DAY FORTY-FOUR, ONE HUNDRED AND FIFTY-TWO CASES, TWELVE DEATHS

It is not easy to convey, unless one has experienced it, the
dramatic feeling of sudden enlightenment that floods the
mind when the right idea finally clicks into place

Francis Crick (discoverer of DNA), 1988

The patients in Block G were getting ready for their afternoon tea break. For once, the ward was not quite full. The two patients who had died had not been replaced by the overspill from Block H. It was considered too risky. The ward was insulated from the continuing crisis in Medenby, and an air of optimism, unduly premature, prevailed. The nurses and health assistants busied themselves, criss-crossing the ward efficiently and silently like ants in a colony, each with a clearly appointed task.

The tea break was a welcome distraction. The trays with tea and biscuits were distributed and voices were no longer muffled. Even Matron Arbuthnot was able to smile as she made her daily round. Perhaps her continued optimism was close to being justified. It might just be true that they were seeing the beginning of the end for Poleaxe.

Stephen Bollider had just visited a ward in the main hospital to see an elderly lady, crippled by fear, who had taken a large overdose of aspirin. She was convinced she must have been infected with Poleaxe and thought that suicide was the best way of avoiding this terrible disease. There was absolutely no possibility that she had come anywhere near someone with the condition. Stephen had tried to convince her that life always meant hope, whereas death abandoned it, but was not sure she had been listening.

By agreement he had been granted a visit to Block H to see the young woman Giles Camberwell had referred. There the building was, dour and unyielding. He entered it, passing by the sign 'DO NOT ENTER'. He identified himself, produced the letter from Dr Camberwell and was allowed to go into the changing room. There he showered and gowned before going into the nursing office.

He checked the name in the notes. 'Barbara Dukinfield'. He read the name aloud. This was always the best way to remember it. He finally entered the ward, looking for Barbara's name at the foot of the bed. Ah, there it was. And how lucky he was. She was clearly the prettiest occupant of Block H, lying on her back, looking innocently at the ceiling.

'Good afternoon, Barbara. My name is Dr Stephen Bollider.'

Barbara was startled to see a new face, or more accurately, a new voice, as the new arrival was largely hidden behind the usual anonymous mask. She felt unsettled again. It was quite terrible losing control of her arms and legs a second time, and she did not want anything to get in the way of recovery.

'Why are you here? Who exactly are you?'

'I am a colleague of Dr Camberwell. He felt it would be helpful if I saw you to make an assessment.'

Barbara was now thoroughly fed up. 'I'm sorry. I have had so many people examining me without any good coming out of it. Prodded and poked, every hole in my body looked into, bits of me removed, machines prying and prowling around my bed, needles everywhere; I just can't tolerate another investigation.' She was close to tears.

'I'm sorry too. I may have used the wrong word. My assessment is different. I just want to talk with you.'

'What do you mean, just talk? How will that help?'

'Can I just ask you to wait and see? Let me know after I've finished. If it all seems useless, I want you to tell me.'

Barbara seemed to be reassured. She nodded. She was beginning to like him. He did not seem perturbed by her irritability.

'First I would like you to tell me how you have been feeling in the past few days.'

'Feeling, in what way?'

Stephen chuckled. 'Yes, feeling is a funny word. I mean feeling in the sense of your emotions, those ups and downs that sometimes seem to be out of control.'

'Pretty awful, really. You see, I was just about to be discharged. Everything was going well and then – out of the blue – I felt this tremendous feeling of panic accompanied by unreality, as though I wasn't here, even though I knew I was. Then I collapsed again, could not remember anything, and when I woke up I had lost the use of my arms and legs again. It was terrifying. They're only just coming back to life.'

'So, just before you collapsed, can you remember how you were feeling?'

'Well, I was excited about going home, even though it is some way off, but,' here Barbara faltered, 'I was also feeling pretty let down.'

Stephen pounced on this. 'Now that's important. What was bothering you?'

Barbara hesitated. She didn't know this man, even though she wanted to trust him. 'May I ask if this conversation is completely confidential?'

Stephen leant forward and held her hand briefly. 'Yes, absolutely. I'm not going to write anything in your notes. This is a private conversation between me and you. I should have told you that I do not work at the hospital, as I am a psychiatrist, and so what I am doing has nothing to do with your medical care here.'

Barbara was both intrigued and annoyed. 'So you have come to see me because you think I'm bonkers?'

'That's a very unfair comment. Dr Camberwell had told me about your symptoms and their possible connection to Poleaxe, so suggested this visit. Talking about your panic and anxiety doesn't make you bonkers any more than your comment about being bonkers makes me feel miserable about our professional image.'

Barbara was chastened and had to make up for it. 'Sorry. If I am being honest, I was feeling completely downhearted because my mother told me about the load of tasks I had to do when I got home, and I didn't think it was fair. She doesn't treat me as an adult. To her, I'm still a little girl who runs after her, does everything she wants and then comes back for more. Sorry to sound like a wimp.' She was crying quietly now.

'So the invalid, if I can call you that, was not being acknowledged. You were terrified that you wouldn't be able to cope?'

'I suppose so, but I was angry, and deflated, too. Mum didn't seem to understand. She wasn't making any allowance for my feelings, or what I had been through. But please, please, don't repeat this to anybody. If Mum knew she would be quite mortified.'

'Mothers often expect too much of their daughters. Both your feelings and hers are quite understandable.'

Barbara seemed puzzled at this curious line of questioning. 'What has this got to do with my disease, then?'

'I'm not exactly sure, but I have an idea. What I would like to do, if you are happy about it, is to come back and do a little experiment. Now, before you get alarmed, by "experiment" I mean talking to you a little more about your emotions and testing how they may affect your body. It might explain why you collapsed when you did, and if it does, we could have ways of preventing it from happening again.'

Barbara was now very intrigued but was not sure how to answer.

Stephen noted her uncertainty. 'I asked at the beginning for you to let me know if my talking was useless. What's your verdict?'

'No, no, no. It certainly hasn't been useless. It's made me think. On reflection, I think I will go through the experiment with you. Nobody else has given me a good explanation for what has been going on, so why not give you a chance?'

But she was not just thinking of the experiment. She wanted to see him again.

FIFTEEN

DAY FORTY-FOUR, ONE HUNDRED AND FIFTY-TWO CASES, TWELVE DEATHS

A new form of neurotic illness is described. Its most consistent features are a combination of depersonalisation and a characteristic form of phobic anxiety

Martin Roth, psychiatrist, 1959

Stephen was pumped up after his meeting with Barbara. On his return to the asylum he went straight into the backroom that served as his study, hardly acknowledging his wife.

Pauline noticed immediately. 'What's going on, darling? You've got a new idea, haven't you? That funny look in your eyes. But please don't get too absorbed. We've got to continue packing for the move.'

Stephen had forgotten about the new house. Packing was not important now. It could wait.

'OK, I haven't forgotten,' he lied. 'Just want to look something up before supper.'

He went straight to one of the papers he had been reading at his postgraduate course. Good, there it was, a paper in 1946 by Dr H Shorvon, with the arresting title of 'The depersonalisation syndrome', presented at the Royal Society of Medicine in 1946.

'Funny, this was just after the war, when everyone was coming back to life, and yet this paper almost describes the opposite.'

Now, what were its key features? There was something that Barbara had told him that had resonated. He ran his fingers down the page.

Ah, there it was, in depersonalisation: 'The experience is distressing and seems to be essentially one of unreality; the world feels unreal; the subject feels he is unreal, totally or partially. They do not say "I am unreal" but "I feel I am not real, although I know that I am".'

Now that was exactly what Barbara had said before she collapsed. She had a tremendous feeling of unreality but knew she was not unreal.

So what else was there in the syndrome: '13 of the 23 cases examined had minor abnormalities in the EEG compared with the standards of normality expected. This percentage abnormality (over 50) is extremely high for any non-organic group.'

So, thought Stephen, *if the brain waves in the EEG were abnormal, there is something pretty abnormal going on in the brain when people get depersonalised.*

He continued reading: 'It is a reversible condition, cases can recover completely and spontaneously. There is a tendency for the disturbance to occur in emotionally immature subjects.'

Now all this seemed to fit Barbara's condition. But what if depersonalisation went one step further? This flash of original thought had to be followed through. He would try something out when he saw Barbara tomorrow.

His thoughts were interrupted by a baby crying.

'Darling, could you do your usual stuff with Patrick?' called Pauline.

Stephen picked up the old, battered copy of *Just So Stories* and went upstairs to the small bedroom. Patrick usually took a little time to get to sleep, so reading to him seemed to be a solution. But reading baby books seemed to leave no impression; he continued mewling and whimpering. So Stephen had given up one evening and read *Just So Stories* instead. This had an instantaneous effect. Jonathan appeared to listen at first. He stopped crying and looked up to the ceiling with unseeing eyes.

Before long the eyelids were beginning to droop.

'For I am the cat that walks by himself, and all places are alike to me,' Stephen intoned in his special lone cat voice, but Patrick was already asleep.

Stephen stayed a little before leaving; he wanted to make sure Patrick was completely asleep. But why was it that an eleven-month-old baby only seemed to acknowledge the words of Rudyard Kipling and not the repetitive simpler stories of Dr Seuss? Could he possibly understand? What was going on in his brain? As he asked himself these questions, he realised that this was why he had decided to specialise in psychiatry. It was the great unknown waiting to be explored, not a well-trodden path to predictability.

He had been one of the brightest students at the University of Sheffield, but when he told his friends and tutors that he wanted to train in mental health, they were universally shocked. The dean of the medical school had even taken him aside and asked him to consider his future.

'I'll be quite frank about this, Stephen. You are one of our brightest stars and I know you would make a brilliant cardiologist. I was hoping you might join me on my firm next year. But of course you can choose what you like. But, heavens above, do not go into psychiatry. It's full of failures who can't get accepted elsewhere and it's a completely unscientific subject. For someone of your intelligence, it would bore you sick.'

'Thank you, Dean, for your concern, but I have already made up my mind. My father always said that I was the most curious of curious paradoxes, as I always seem to go in what seems to be the wrong direction. That's probably why I came to Sheffield to train, even though I had a place at St Thomas's Hospital in London.' This was a good way of ending this particular conversation and the dean dutifully gave up trying.

But Stephen still had some doubts about his choice. He was ambitious to make his mark in the subject. The great unknown of mental illness needed to be mapped out in more detail, but he was not sure where to start. And although the dean at Sheffield was wrong about psychiatry, he was partly right in his conclusions that those who chose it were not the most dynamic of colleagues. Far too many of them acted like the former members of the profession. They were called alienists, as they, secure in their asylums, were only on the fringe of medicine. Many liked the quiet lifestyle, with relatively little in the way of emergencies, ample accommodation on site, meals whenever you wanted them, and the prospect of early retirement at the age of fifty-five, since for some reason psychiatry was felt to be a stressful profession so you were allowed to leave early. Stephen had seen very little of stress in his colleagues and a quite considerable helping of laziness, but perhaps Middleshire Hospital was atypical.

As for Pauline, she was doing very well in general practice and had already made quite a name for herself with her productive ideas. He could see there was a danger that he could be left behind in their friendly but highly competitive relationship, so he needed a fillip to restore his status.

Yes, Patrick was now completely asleep. As Stephen tiptoed downstairs, he was thinking that he might be able to catch up a little on his wife, and on his other medical colleagues, if he followed up these hunches without the diversion of doubt. But of course he would also have to convince the other doctors at Medenby Hospital if he was to make further progress.

SIXTEEN

DAY FIFTY, ONE HUNDRED AND FIFTY-FOUR CASES, TWELVE DEATHS

The will to win, the desire to succeed, the urge to reach your full potential... these are the keys that will unlock the door to personal excellence

Confucius, 494 BC

James was ready to give good news to the Poleaxe Task Group. He was now brimming with the self-confidence of a champion, had arrived early and set out his papers carefully in advance. He was standing and smiling as the others shuffled in: Charles Merridew in brown corduroys, William Fothergill in his trademark dark grey suit, Archie Patterson in his usual white lab coat (he would not dress up for anybody) and Christopher Barclay in his brown tweeds. Harry Berry, James's deputy, was also at the meeting. He had only just started his post and was very green, but he had been diligent in all his work, so he had been honoured with an invitation. Madeleine Bishop was seated next to him, now wearing a patterned smock dress and looking more confident than usual. James was pleased that his nurturing was yielding results.

'Good news, ladies and gentlemen. We have had no new cases outside the Medenby exclusion zone in the past week and only two within it, so it looks, (a) as though our blockade is working, and (b) the people of Medenby are following our advice to avoid unnecessary contact with each other.'

William was fulsome in his reply. James had expected this, as the Fothergill psyche depended greatly on flattering people when they were up and kicking them unmercifully when they were down. 'That is very impressive, James. It certainly looks as though we have broken the back of this and your strategy is working. Obviously we have a long way to go before all is completely elucidated, but if we continue in this vein I am sure morale will rise enormously.' William had a way of saying the obvious as though it comprised original thought.

But James could not be unseemly and bask in praise. 'Can I ask Madeleine and Harry to give the latest news about the outbreak so we know exactly where we are?'

Madeleine stood up. There was really no need to stand up, but she was sure it gave her statements more authority.

'We still think that the first infected person is likely to be Julia Unwincroft. She was in Singapore before travelling by sea back to England and we think she must have picked up the infection there. We now have a clear pattern of transmission for all the people affected – it is by the respiratory route. Harry has a graph which shows the clusters of all the 154 people affected and these all stem from the original contact in the park.'

Harry unrolled a large drawing of what looked like spiderwebs superimposed on a map of Medenby. 'Not all people were affected immediately, but once we take account of this variation it is clear that all these clusters link to one of the original group who were first infected. The cases outside Medenby involved people who had visited the town and had contact with at least one of these clusters. The isolation of the town now seems to have stopped, or at least seriously deterred, further spread. But there are some puzzling features that Madeleine will explain.'

Madeleine stood up again. 'What we do find a little odd is that many people have not suffered from the syndrome even though they have almost certainly been exposed to infection. One person was in a meeting at a crowded pub and of the thirty people who were there, only three developed Poleaxe symptoms. This is odd, as if this syndrome is new it would be expected to infect many more.'

'There is such a thing as natural immunity,' droned Charles.

'I appreciate that, but it looks as though in other groups it has been much more infectious. Some people attending a MIND meeting in the town all got the syndrome from one person who was only there for ten minutes.'

'What exactly is MIND?' asked Archie.

'It's a mental health charity,' replied Madeleine. 'It promotes community care for the mentally ill.'

'We don't want too much of that in the town at present,' scoffed William. 'We would have a real epidemic on our hands if they were all let loose.'

James needed to move on. 'The infection now seems to be under control, but are we any closer to the cause?'

Charles was now in his element. 'We can be quite certain what it is not. It is not Japanese encephalitis or any variant of this, as this is transmitted by mosquitoes, who, to the best of my knowledge, are not exactly flourishing in Medenby.'

A few glanced at the drizzle outside and smiled. This was the nearest Charles got to humour.

'The post-mortem examination of the brains of those who have died show inclusions in the brain that are typical of viral diseases. But they are not specific, so do not help us to make an identification.'

Archibald Patterson was determined to add a sour contribution, and all would have been disappointed had he not risen to his normal level of discontent. 'There are still too many questions left unanswered. The post-mortem findings do not really tell us anything, apart from the vague suggestion a virus is the likely infective agent. We have no idea where the infection has come from, where it is going to go, and how many more will be affected. A mystery controlled is not a mystery solved.'

James had to snuff out these observations from the predictable doom merchant. 'These are still early days, Archie. What we need to do is to prevent the spread of the disease so it is confined to the smallest possible area. Now that the number of new cases is getting less with every succeeding day we have a measure of our success. Ignorance of cause is a worry, but I know you will agree that once we have no more people coming down with Poleaxe we are at least halfway there.'

'James is right,' added William. 'There are dozens of diseases where we do not have full answers about their

97

exact nature but know enough to be confident about their occurrence. And anyway, Archie, it is up to you chaps in the microbiology field to give us the real answers, so I hope your friends in Colindale will soon tell us what is really going on with Poleaxe.'

'I think we all owe a vote of thanks to James and his public health team,' added Dr Barclay with his usual generosity. 'Only two weeks ago everybody here was in a state of wild panic. We were being overrun by an illness that was out of control and completely unpredictable. Now it is boxed in, has few options to escape, and everything has settled down. I even get the impression that the people of Medenby like their new status in the world, so everybody seems to be getting positives from what at first appeared to be a total mess and a likely tragedy.'

The meeting continued, with its predictable discussions about the supply of medicines, ambulance access and plans to both extend and reduce the numbers in the isolation wards. Here James was happy to let William to take over the meeting while he sat back, observing their interactions with quiet amusement, knowing he had made his mark on the establishment that had for too long found him easy to ignore. Poleaxe had certainly been a godsend to him. The marvellous process of random had deposited it on Medenby, or perhaps it was Providence. Certainly without it, he would be still be just one of many medical officers of health working quietly and anonymously, unappreciated but necessary disease preventers and protectors. Now he was at the forefront, and he was determined to stay there. Standard bearers should be properly exalted and not be deposed until their work was done.

SEVENTEEN

DAY FIFTY-ONE, ONE HUNDRED AND FIFTY-FOUR CASES, TWELVE DEATHS

Science is nothing but trained and organised common sense

TH Huxley, 1880

Stephen was ready to carry out his experiment with Barbara. He had arrived early at Block H. He was now able to slip through the administrative hoops at the entrance by charming the nurse. His mental hospital garb was always ripe for a joke.

'Men in white coats arriving again to take you away; you're in competition with us now.' Soon, he, gowned and sterile, but with no need for a mask now, was perched on a chair by Barbara's bed.

Barbara had been nervous, ruminating in anticipation after waking early. But she was also excited. When she thought about why, it was not just the thought of the experiment. It was the thought of meeting Stephen again. He was handsome in a curious sort of way, with his earnest face, his puckered brow, his gentle hands. She wanted to feel them on her body again. He was professional, but also down to earth, and she liked that.

'This experiment, if we can call it that, is just to try and recreate the circumstances before you collapsed. But to do that I would like to take both the times you first collapsed in the park, and the one after you met your parents, together, to see if there are any common factors.'

But Barbara needed more than procedure, she wanted to know the purpose, and she wanted this interview to last. 'What exactly do you want to do, and what is likely to happen? I don't want to be just a guinea pig to satisfy you.' She turned her face to look at him directly and noticed, with pleasure, that he blushed. She had rehearsed these standard questions directly and was confident of getting straight answers. What had he to hide?

Stephen was torn. He did not want to say too much. He had reasons to believe Barbara would be cooperative but did not want disclose too much about his ideas at this point. So he reverted to analogy. 'Have you any pets at home?'

'Yes, we have a black Labrador, Cerby.'

'Nice name.'

'Yes, she was the smallest of nine pups, so we had to call her Cerberus.'

'Glad to know you are aware of life on Mount Olympus. And does Cerby ever have odd behaviour, like wetting herself or chasing her tail?'

'Yes, she does wet herself, very occasionally.'

'And do you know when she is going to wet herself?'

'Not exactly, it could be because she's had pups or because at times she gets excited.'

'Yes, but you don't know which. But if you made a record of the circumstances at all the times she wet herself you might know better what the reason was. That's why I want to take both your occasions together. And if there are more we might be able to distinguish a pattern.'

Barbara concluded this logic was reasonable. She had come across similar problems in her anthropology studies. 'All right. But I'll be surprised if you find a link.'

So she described, as best she could, about the first time she had collapsed in the park, even though it was all very hazy. She then recounted the second time when Pamela and Robert were visiting. She was careful not to criticise either of them, but Stephen seemed to detect some annoyance with Pamela from her description – something she found it hard to disguise. She then mentioned a third occasion when she was told that one of her close friends had developed Poleaxe. She was very distressed by this and found her legs were leaden and could hardly move them. But she was in bed and the feeling disappeared soon afterwards so she had told nobody.

Stephen was obviously impressed by the care with which she responded. He took her into his confidence. 'What I wondered, and it may be completely crazy to say so, is that the second and third time you had these symptoms you were very distressed, anxious, worried, whatever you like to call it, and this may have brought on the attack.'

'You may be right.' Barbara was now very intrigued. 'You may be interested in something else too. When I have talked to all the people in the ward who have had Poleaxe, they all seem to be like me, nervous types. I couldn't work out if it was all because of Poleaxe or whether they had always been nervous. So I got hold of the crazy idea that only nervous people get the Poleaxe symptoms and, while they still have the disease, when they get really panicky and highly anxious, the symptoms can come on again.'

Stephen was amazed by the interest and awareness that Barbara had shown in understanding Poleaxe. Whatever else the disease had done to her, it had not stopped her brain working well. It was clear she could become a valuable assistant, as she was on the ward, had made friends with many of the other patients and was very observant. So she could find out how many of the patients on the ward were naturally over-anxious. He wondered if she could also give questionnaires to the patients. Some of them measured anxiety proneness, the tendency to be anxious all the time, and it would be interesting to know how the Poleaxe patients compared with others.

Stephen was impressed by Barbara's thinking. She had formulated the hypothesis that he had been generating and was expressing it much better than him. He almost hugged her, but jerked backwards when he realised this would be most improper on the ward.

Barbara, her anthropological antennae fully operational, detected his movement towards her and wished he had continued. He would be a good hugger.

'Well, Barbara. We are certainly of like mind. I had exactly the same idea about Poleaxe being linked to nervousness before I came to see you today. I had thought I might try an experiment using hypnosis to see if your symptoms could be altered by changing your level of anxiety. But this may not be necessary, and it could be risky.'

Barbara was having none of this. The excitement she was feeling made entirely unbothered by risk. 'No, no. I think this is a marvellous idea. I really would like to know if this funny disease is affected by emotion. I should tell you that I am an anthropology student and it's helped me to understand that anxiety and all those other emotional feelings are much more important in cultures other than our own. So, I'm prepared to go ahead. If you wanted to, you could say it's connected to one of my research projects, as it would be at least partly true.' She looked up at him, half pleading.

Stephen was convinced. Who could not be persuaded by this winsome young lady with the inviting eyes? 'All right. Let's do it. But Barbara, in doing this experiment I am going to adopt a different approach. I want you to listen carefully to what I am saying and not to take any notice of how I am saying it. Just listen very carefully to my voice. There is no need to interrupt or ask any questions.'

Barbara dutifully settled down and listened. Stephen's voice altered, becoming monotonous but seductive. Barbara wriggled beneath the bedclothes in anticipation, noticing her breasts were firmer and her breathing more rapid.

'Barbara, I want you to listen to me and ignore everything else. While you are listening, you will find yourself getting more and more relaxed, more and more relaxed, feeling heavy and comfortable, just listening to the sound of my voice.'

Barbara complied. This was not at all difficult, as his voice was very soothing and she could almost imagine Stephen being in bed beside her. His voice almost seemed to be stroking her body.

Stephen continued, 'Now you are fully relaxed, could you raise your arms and bend your knees slowly.'

Barbara complied. This was going to be fun.

'Now lower your arms and raise them again in time with my voice. Also do the same with your knees. Up and down, up and down slowly, breathing in time with my voice.'

Barbara luxuriated in her ready responses. She no longer had any anxiety. Stephen was a very good therapist. She drifted off into some sort of alternative space where everything was calm. He watched her closely but continued repeating his instructions. Finally he passed his hand very slowly over her face but there was no response. She was hypnotised enough.

Now was the time to switch tack.

'And now it's time for you to wake up and leave, Barbara, as you are needed at home. This is very important.'

His voice had changed. Harsh and pressured.

'You are needed at home. There are things to do there and if you are not at home something may go badly wrong. Nobody else is going to be able to help. So you can no longer be resting here. There is much to be done. So please wake up – immediately.'

There was a short pause. Barbara opened her eyes. She looked puzzled. 'Where am I?' she asked in a nervous, girly voice, turning her head towards Stephen, who found her full lips and oval face framed by her long brown hair disconcerting and irritatingly attractive.

'You are in Medenby Hospital, Barbara. I want you to raise your arms and bend your knees for me, now.'

Barbara tried, and tried again. 'I can't. They won't move. They honestly won't move. Am I dreaming, or am I awake? What is going on? Is all this real?'

Stephen reverted to his normal voice, well-modulated but very clear. 'I have just hypnotised you, Barbara, as I wanted to find out how you, and in particular, your body, would react to you becoming anxious. So I want to know exactly how you are feeling now.'

'It's like I said before. I feel cut off. It's though I'm not here, I'm away from reality and my legs and arms have left me too. Don't tell me. I've got Poleaxe again.' In spite of all her wish to help, she was now ready to cry.

'Listen to me very closely, Barbara. Remember what I was saying earlier. You were listening very carefully to me. I want you to join me again, getting relaxed again, feeling heavy and comfortable, sinking into the bed, listening only to the sound of my voice.'

Barbara needed no invitation to return to her state of nirvana. Normal wakefulness was much more disturbing. She was soon close to slumber but retained the feeling of calm that was normally so alien to her. It was worth staying in this state just awake to remind her of its warmth.

When Stephen felt Barbara was completely relaxed, he changed his voice again. 'I want you to slowly wake up now, Barbara. Very slowly, listening only to the sound of my voice. As you wake up, you are feeling better, more relaxed but also comfortable and content. I am going to count from one to ten, and when I reach the number "ten", I want you to open your eyes and look at me.'

He counted, '…eight, nine, ten.'

Barbara opened her eyes, smiling at him. She felt ridiculously and stupidly content, and wanted to freeze the moment.

'Now, Barbara, I would like you to raise your arms and flex your knees.'

Barbara did so, effortlessly.

'But a few minutes ago you could not move them at all.'

She then did something she had never done before and might probably never do again in such a public place as a hospital ward. Perhaps it was something to do with the hypnotism. She leant forward, showing really much too much of her slender, creamy body to Stephen, and gave him the big hug she had wanted before.

'You've done it, you have really done it. You've solved the Poleaxe problem.'

Nurse Grant was curious to know what was going on by Barbara's bed. It was rather different from a normal visit. 'Is anything wrong, Barbara? You seem a little excited.'

'Of course I am, we have just found out what starts off Poleaxe and keeps it going. Meet our local expert, Dr Stephen Bollider, and he will tell you more.'

EIGHTEEN

DAY FIFTY-THREE, NO NEW CASES, NO NEW DEATHS

I have a kind of self resides with you;
But an unkind self, that itself will leave,
To be another's fool

William Shakespeare, *Troilus and Cressida*, 1609

Stephen knocked on the door of James Porton's office in Lombard Street in Medenby. There was no bell, and the door and its surrounds were getting grubby. James, dressed in a dark grey suit and waistcoat in advance of his meeting with William Fothergill later that day, greeted him at the door.

'Good of you to see me,' said Stephen, 'as you know, I've come about the Poleaxe problem.'

James was on edge. Unfamiliar people, especially doctors, asking about Poleaxe, bothered him. Everything was going well; there was no reason for any disturbance. He liked to be sure of his territory, so he wanted a short interview.

'I am very busy, as you might imagine, so I hope your enquiry can be brief.'

Stephen dived in; he needed to get his point over and there was clearly little time. 'I'm a psychiatrist in training at Middleshire Hospital who has seen a few cases of Poleaxe. I've been conducting some enquiries.'

James interrupted irritably. 'What exactly do you mean, "conducting enquiries"? You're only a junior psychiatrist, I understand.'

'Yes, but I've spent a great deal of time examining a few patients and think their mental state has something to do with their symptoms. I've found that I can induce some of the symptoms when I put the patients under some kinds of stress.'

'And what exactly do you mean by "stress" in this context?'

'I know this is an overused term, but it seems that when people with this Poleaxe condition are placed, mentally, in stressful situations that replicate the ones when they first got unwell, under some circumstances they can have a minor relapse.'

James was now alarmed and very irritated indeed. 'Do you mean to tell me, young man, that you have been seeing these very ill people in hospital, who are only just beginning to recover from their terrible ordeal, and carrying out psychological experiments on them?'

'They are not experiments in the conventional sense; I have just been exploring their emotions. One of the people I have seen, Barbara Dukinfield, has been very helpful in explaining her own feelings, and she developed this idea first.'

James now felt he had to respond harshly to this whippersnapper. He had to get rid of him – and make sure he did not come back. 'I don't know what you've been doing, Dr Bollider, and what your motives are. Poleaxe has absolutely nothing to do with you. I suggest you go straight back to Middleshire Hospital and turn your attention towards your proper job of looking after the ill patients you have there. It is way out of order for you to be going into our isolation wards and interfering with patients who have this serious disease. You are putting both them and yourself at risk.'

He could see that Stephen was annoyed. Good. He now needed to scare him off. This man should not be interfering with the Poleaxe enquiry. It was already complicated enough without interferers from outside. But Stephen was standing firm.

'I have come here in good faith to ask you to consider another aspect of this condition. All I am asking you is to think about making full assessments of the mental health of these people, as this may help your enquiries. Ignoring the subject is simply not good enough.'

James's message was not getting through. He decided to become furious; he was quite good at fury, and it normally worked. 'I am not going to listen to your impudence one moment longer. Please leave this office immediately. I am going to report you to Dr Fothergill and your supervisor – Dr Wattis, I think it is – and ask them to ban you from coming to Blocks G and H until further notice.'

He stood up and banged a paperweight on the table to emphasise his fury. Stephen was already half out of the room and it was only when he turned to close the door that he saw the papers James had disturbed slowly floating to the ground. James, still standing, stared aggressively at Stephen as he left, and stayed in this position until the outer door had closed and he was sure that this visitor from the asylum had been emptied of all contact.

He sat back in his chair and reflected on his performance. He had handled the interview badly in that he was rude, but he was pleased that he had pulled rank in talking to a junior who was clearly out of his depth. But he could not understand why people who came from mental health settings always annoyed him. It was such a wishy-washy subject; it never went anywhere. And clearly it had nothing to do with Poleaxe.

Nevertheless, he should at least have let this young doctor have his say without dismissing him as a nobody. But his instincts were correct. All this mental stress stuff was an irrelevance and he must nip it in the bud. Poleaxe needed science, not opinion, and psychiatry was opinion dressed up as science. This Dr Bollider needed to be kept away from the isolation wards. He would phone William Fothergill immediately and write to Dr Wattis too. Poleaxe should be placed out of bounds to interlopers who would only confuse rather than clarify.

NINETEEN

DAY FIFTY-THREE, NO NEW CASES, NO NEW DEATHS

Prejudices, it is well known, are most difficult to eradicate from the heart whose soil has never been loosened or fertilised by education: they grow there, firm as weeds among stones

Charlotte Brontë, 1847

Stephen drove back to Middleshire Hospital past the roadblocks. He was even more angry than at the end of the interview. This Porton fellow would have to be brought down to size. Prejudice should never handcuff science, and prejudice against mental illness was rife in the medical profession. He had to make an appointment to see Dr Wattis as soon as possible before this popinjay of public health was able to spin a story that would sabotage further enquiry about the real causes of the Poleaxe Syndrome. Whatever happened now, he was not going to give up. Barbara and he may be right about their theory, or they might be wrong, but the hypothesis needed to be tested.

But his anger with James Porton could not be contained. He had been denied a voice, and that was unconscionable. No attempt had been made to listen to his ideas; he had been dismissed as an ignoramus who knew nothing about medicine, and Porton had been insufferably rude. Whilst he was used to psychiatrists being belittled, this behaviour took it to a new level. There was an obvious answer. He would need to publish his findings quickly and let the world decide if he was right. But first he needed to see Dr Wattis for advice.

Good. He was in his office and welcomed Stephen warmly.

'I'm very sorry to disturb you at such short notice, but I've had the most awful meeting with James Porton.'

Stephen sat down and breathed heavily. He retold the encounter with James, adding the words 'smug', 'self-satisfied' and 'arrogant' at intervals along the way.

David listened carefully until Stephen had finished. He had noticed that he clearly needed to ventilate his anger; there was no point in interrupting. Then he spoke quietly but firmly. 'Let's look at it from Dr Porton's point of view. He's been running the Poleaxe show for a few weeks now. He seems to be getting on top of it as the number of cases is falling. You appearing on his doorstep without much warning and tossing a new theory into the ring has thrown him off balance. If someone suddenly came into my office and claimed that half the patients in my ward really had medical rather than mental illnesses I would probably get equally aerated.'

'I guess so. But he cannot suppress new evidence.'

'No,' observed David, smiling wryly, 'but you will know from the doctors here from the Soviet Union that some people can make a pretty good job of it.'

Stephen had met some of these psychiatrists, whom David had generously offered attachments to escape the dead hand of mental health in the communist bloc, and appreciated the point.

'But we are a free country, and the truth must come out eventually. And in this case it needs to come out sooner. I may have got some things wrong, but what I have to say may save lives. Do you agree that I need to publish my findings, because they are relevant to the mystery of a disease like Poleaxe that appears to have come from nowhere?'

It was obvious that David was on Stephen's side here, but he wanted to steer him towards a measured response rather than a foolish one that might only antagonise.

'I agree, but if you are too strident, your words will fall on deaf ears. Look, I know you are itching to get back at Porton, but be very careful not to let your personal feelings come into your arguments. If you just state your findings soberly, indicating that there is likely to be an unacknowledged mental health component to Poleaxe, you will have done enough. Can I suggest a letter to the *BMJ*, you know, the *British Medical Journal*, as this is read by all doctors?'

Stephen protested that this would not give him enough space to argue his point, but David rammed the point home. 'What you have told me can be summarised in five hundred words at most; you do not need more. And,' here he paused, as he understood Stephen would not like his work to be over-controlled by others, 'could you let me have a look at what you have written before you submit?'

'Of course,' replied Stephen, somewhat surprised, as David had not shown much interest in his work before.

The phone rang. David picked it up. 'Is Dr Bollider with you? He is needed urgently for the medication review in Lily Ward.' Stephen heard this too, rose and left swiftly, with a nodded thanks. Back to earth with a medication review.

As he left the headquarters building he was deflated but determined, and on reflection realised the wisdom of David's advice. Being a psychiatrist was like being in the third division of medicine. At the top were the respected physicians and surgeons, who could point to their successes in terms of lives saved or turned around, followed by their attendant specialists in pathology, radiology, haematology and other disciplines that could back up clinical decisions with tests whose results were accepted as absolute fact. He, and other psychiatrists, had no other assets apart from their clinical skills. They were not treating people who would die without care, unless it was by suicide, and evidence for their success here was mediocre, and they had no independent tests to show their success. So they remained in the third division, tolerated by some and derided by many 'shrinks', 'quacks' and 'trick-cyclists', who staggered across the medical stage as jesters and fools, preparing the audience for the serious action to come.

Stephen made his way down the winding path to Lily Ward at the far end of the hospital. The ward was hardly part of Middleshire Hospital's shop window, so its distant position allowed it to be delicately bypassed on official visits. Stephen had overheard one of these.

'And that building over there,' the over-inquisitive lady mayor had asked. 'What is that for?'

'Oh, I think it's a storehouse,' the chairman of the Regional Health Committee had responded, probably believing his own fiction.

As Stephen approached the long, squat grey-white building, he was greeted by a small elderly woman, walking briskly towards him in a grey apron. 'Morning to you, Dr Bollider, lovely reminder of summer. Don't let that Poleaxe spoil it.'

Stephen nodded. 'No, it won't,' he replied inaccurately, 'but don't work too hard in the laundry. You must get out and enjoy the good weather when it comes.' He knew Phyllis Ollerenshaw well. He could not understand at first why she was in the hospital but knew immediately once he had read her clinical records.

She had been admitted to Middleshire Hospital in 1920 when her new-born baby was found dead. There was not enough evidence to convict Phyllis of murder, but in any case, she was said to be 'mentally deranged' at trial and so was committed to the hospital. She had been there ever since, but it was clear from her notes that she had recovered very quickly, almost certainly from post-natal depression. But in the 1920s there was nowhere for her to go if she was discharged. So she stayed in the hospital, and as she was so well she was set to work in the hospital laundry. She was clearly very able and had gradually been promoted to a senior supervisory position. But of course, mental hospital patients had no official retirement age, so here she was, forty-five years later, still working full-time at the age of sixty-eight. Stephen could not make up his mind whether she was a disgustingly exploited victim of a failed medical system or a happy woman who had found a comfortable niche in life through unexpected circumstances.

He was almost at the entrance. *Lily Ward*, he said to himself. *Why are the most unattractive places in life given the names of beautiful flowers?* It was an insult to nature. The ward was gaunt and gloomy, with many of the curtains drawn during the day. The air always smelt of stale urine. Hollow cries and moans funnelled down the aisle between the aged bedsteads, and when there was the occasional laughter it degenerated into hysterical cackling.

As he walked down the ward, a hand was slipped into his. A soft, husky voice murmured, 'Dr Bolly, when are we to be married?' Stephen knew immediately on touch that this was Hermione, the siren of Lily Ward, who had attracted the diagnosis of erotomania, the pathological infatuation of the desperately available with the securely unattainable.

He looked down to see Hermione's imploring face, which would have been more attractive if it had not been so liberally endowed with lipstick. 'There have been some delays, Hermione, but I will let you know.' The nurses had advised him to go along with Hermione's dream, as her behaviour on the ward had been so much better with romance, but he was finding the pretence difficult.

The medication review was the usual farce. The most important requirement of the nurses seemed to be keeping the ward quiet at night. They battled with Stephen to increase sedation in the evening, whilst he was equally determined to have the patients fully conscious by day. But with forty patients in the ward, it was not possible to assess them all adequately and frequently he was ground under.

As he returned to the hospital flat, he looked forward to the day when his family could move back into a normal world with a house of their own. Some of his colleagues were like Phyllis. They liked the security of the mental hospital: the regular stodgy meals, the flimsy confidence that comes with having little responsibility in organising the necessities of life and a passive journey towards retirement that squeezed out ambition with each succeeding year. He shuddered at the thought that he might follow in their path.

This seemed light years away from his argument about Poleaxe with Dr Porton. He laughed at himself when thinking of the possible implications. If the condition was a purely mental one, all the patients could be shuffled off to Middleshire and other mental hospitals, where their fates could conveniently be forgotten. The Victorian philosophy guiding the creation of these hospitals far away in the country, 'out of sight, out of mind', had a tragic logic that could not be denied. And when he recalled David Wattis's advice, he could understand why Porton had been so dismissive. How could someone like Stephen, a junior doctor in an outlying part of medicine that was so distant from ordinary practice that its exponents used to be called 'alienists', challenge the giants in their hospital fortresses?

But Stephen was an optimist, and he soon dismissed these defeatist notions. Mental and physical illness were joined at the hip. Their separation over the last thousand years was a combination of ignorant bureaucracy, medical snobbery and arrant prejudice. He could be at the forefront of bringing them together again; he had to be. But first he had to convince the *BMJ* that Poleaxe was not a straightforward medical disease and that the results of his simple experiments showed this unequivocally. He would get writing this evening, once Patrick had learnt from Rudyard Kipling how the elephant had got its trunk.

TWENTY

DAY FIFTY-SIX, ONE NEW CASE, NO NEW DEATHS

Every line we succeed in publishing today – no matter how uncertain the future to which we entrust it – is a victory wrenched from the powers of darkness

Walter Benjamin, 1937

Stephen knew what to do. He was an aspiring psychiatrist and knew he could not make any name for himself without getting published in a learned journal. 'Publish or perish' was a common mantra in academia and he was not going to contradict it. But he had to be careful not to overstate his findings, and also be aware that he, as a junior member of the profession, would have a harder task to persuade editorial staff to approve publication.

But he had no doubt where he ought to publish. The *British Medical Journal*, often abbreviated simply to the *BMJ*, was the right place. Almost every doctor in the country received this journal and it received massive press coverage. He agreed with David Wattis: if he wrote his findings as a letter rather than a full article, it would also be more likely to be published.

Pauline agreed with him too. She had already had several papers published in general practice journals and was more experienced than he was in the field.

'You've got to get the title right,' she said. 'If the title's boring, you're done for. Nobody will read what's below. But it must be accurate too. If you wrote "Poleaxe is a mental disorder, not a physical one", you would certainly get the full attention of the reader, but the text would contradict the title. The editors would pick this up immediately and throw the paper out.'

So Stephen knew he had to choose his words very carefully. He also wanted to avoid any form of jargon, as it was important for his letter to be understood easily by all readers, whether they be general practitioners, psychiatrists, physicians or the general public. So he would write clearly, and follow George Orwell's advice to avoid hackneyed phrases, as they were like a 'packet of aspirins always at one's elbow', and to use short words rather than long ones. After five attempts he had a version ready to submit:

Poleaxe: the mental part of a physical disease

Sir: the cause of Poleaxe is still not known. At present it is thought to be a physical disease, probably an infection. I wish to report findings that suggest a mental component also. These are based on interviews and assessments of twelve patients at Medenby Hospital who had the Poleaxe

Syndrome. I gave the Taylor Manifest Anxiety Scale (TMAS) to each of them after they had recovered from the acute form of the disease. I also gave the scale to eight other patients in the hospital who had recently recovered from myocardial infarction. As much as possible I gave the TMAS questionnaire to the patients after similar duration of in-patient stays. All the patients had been in hospital for at least two weeks but not longer than six weeks.

The mean scores for the Poleaxe patients was 26.2 (sd 3.7) and 16.5 (sd 4.1) for the cardiac patients, a highly significant difference (P<0.01).

There are two ways to interpret these results. The TMAS, despite its name, measures trait anxiety, a general predisposition to anxiety, rather than manifest or actual anxiety at interview. It could be argued that Poleaxe is a more anxiety-provoking condition than a myocardial infarction as its cause is currently unknown. But myocardial infarction is likely to have a higher death rate. It may be equally, or more, anxiogenic. The second explanation, that high anxiety levels are a precursor of affliction by Poleaxe, is a more likely one. The uniformly high levels of trait anxiety in the Poleaxe victims is striking.

Further evidence that anxiety is relevant in the symptomatology of Poleaxe comes from an experiment carried out on one of the patients, with her approval. Under hypnosis the patient was brought into a state of high anxiety and developed the paralytic symptoms of Poleaxe at this time, only for them to disappear when her anxiety levels returned to normal.

I conclude that anxiety is an important component of the Poleaxe Syndrome and is a potential cause rather than a consequence of the disease. This requires further investigation.

He was happy with this. Of course, Barbara should have been a co-author, but as she was a patient rather than a doctor, this would not go down well with the journal, and so she had to be left out.

He showed the letter to Pauline.

'Not bad at all; I'll give you the George Orwell prize for clarity. You've kept it short and pithy but included all the important elements. You've stated the facts, provided explanations, and not gone beyond the data. It is now for the world to take it forward.'

But there was one more task to do. David Wattis had to check the text. He knew it was urgent and had asked him to bring it over to the physician superintendent's house once he had finished. It was just outside the grounds, an impressive Edwardian building with a fine rose garden behind. Stephen could now see some advantages in the alienist way of life.

David met him at the front door and quickly read the letter. 'That's just right. It's clear to me you have a bright future as an author. Doctors who can write are in high esteem. Send it off straight away.'

Stephen had anticipated this. He folded the paper, placed it in the envelope he had brought with him and addressed to the editor at the *BMJ*. His hands shook a little as he sealed it. His first publication was a milestone in his career. He hoped this short letter would be the first of many of the contributions he would make to science. What was more, once published, it would be a permanent record for centuries to come. That was special. He went from David's house to the letterbox at the end of the road. It was too important to go through the hospital mail. The postal service, despite all the confusion of Poleaxe, was still highly reliable. And once he had heard the letter drop through the familiar red box, his satisfaction was complete.

TWENTY-ONE

DAY SIXTY-FOUR, ONE NEW CASE, NO NEW DEATHS

Right is right, and wrong is wrong, and a body ain't got no business doing wrong when he ain't ignorant and knows better

Mark Twain, 1884

Stephen had just completed a visit to a day hospital to the north of Medenby and was on his way to the Ethics Committee meeting. It had been a relatively easy journey through Checkpoint C (the Castle Road entrance). The barrier had now, predictably, been renamed Checkpoint Charlie, and one wit had already stuck up a notice – 'YOU ARE NOW ENTERING THE AMERICAN SECTOR' – at the Medenby entrance.

Stephen was not looking forward to this meeting. He had a strong case to defend, but it was difficult to overcome bias when it preceded him. He noticed the registration of the large Rover P5 in the consultants' car park, LEN 1. That must be the car belonging to Leonard Edwin Nolan, the chair of the Ethics Committee. Trust him to have a personalised number plate; it revealed much about his personality. Although he understood Leonard worked part-time as a consultant dermatologist at the hospital, he noted that his other role was as a barrister. *So a legal grilling awaits*, thought Stephen when he checked on his adversary, *but at least I have not broken the law.*

He had planned the defence of his actions carefully. Poleaxe was an unknown disease, all possible causes had to be considered, and everybody had to suspend preconceived judgments. Stephen thought of himself as a researcher, but equally he could argue that everybody involved in the care of the Poleaxe patients was a research worker too. Anything unusual had to be noted and examined. The most obscure of signals could point the direction to the cause and cure.

He also had his self-confidence reinforced by the letter he had received from the *British Medical Journal* this very morning, confirming they were going to publish his letter about Poleaxe. He would not mention this, but its knowledge stiffened his purpose; he was not going to be pushed around. He entered the main building and went into the Committee Room. What a long table; it seemed to extend far into the distance. Everyone was seated. All were men.

Odd, thought Stephen, *are women unable to consider ethical issues? Perhaps these stalwarts of good practice consider them too emotional.* In front of each of them there was a full glass of water. *No doubt*, Stephen thought wryly, *because their discussions are so dry.*

A rosy-faced, sandy-haired man sat at the end of the table. Stephen noted the unnecessarily large table sign in front of him: 'DR LEONARD NOLAN, Chair (Medenby Ethical Committee)'. He looked through Stephen rather than at him.

'Thank you, Dr Bollider, you may sit down.'

Stephen had already sat down, and smiled sweetly at Leonard.

'We have asked to see you because we consider your recent behaviour in Block G to constitute unethical conduct unworthy of a medical doctor.'

Stephen was about to protest, but Leonard held up his hand. 'I will ask Peggy Beetwood, our secretary, to read out the charge.'

Peggy, a middle-aged ox-like woman, stood up and read in a stentorian voice, 'On 24th April 1967, you, without approval from Dr Fothergill, Dr Porton or any other responsible medical officer, examined a patient under the care of the Poleaxe team in Block H. You then proceeded to carry out an experiment, despite having no prior permission to do so, on a patient, Miss BD, that led to her collapsing in the ward and having to be resuscitated by nursing staff. The staff in Block G, together with Dr Porton and Dr Fothergill, consider that your irresponsible actions put a patient in grave danger. We are therefore minded to report you to the General Medical Council.'

Peggy sat down heavily. The table shook slightly.

'How do you respond to this charge, Dr Bollider?' Leonard asked.

Stephen was expecting him to plead 'guilty' or 'not guilty' so was pleased that he was at least allowed an explanation. He was going to argue it as much as possible without unnecessary emotion, but the threat of being reported to the General Medical Council was alarming.

'I have three comments to make in response. I was asked to see this patient by a medical colleague, Dr Camberwell, and I considered him to have approved the referral. He felt there was a mental health component to her Poleaxe disorder and, quite understandably, wanted a psychiatric opinion. Secondly, after I saw her, and expressly asked her permission and gave her time to reflect, she allowed me to carry out an experiment to alter her mental state. I had surmised from my research this might simulate the Poleaxe Syndrome.

'The experiment was successful and confirmed, in main part, the hypothesis I had developed, and my other enquiries support this too. My conclusion is that other patients with the Poleaxe Syndrome would respond similarly if so tested.'

Leonard was getting more red-faced as Stephen made his case. This was not going to be a pushover, but he hoped at least others might be listening.

'I ask you to confine yourself to the ethical issue at hand, Dr Bollider. You are not delivering a lecture. These are the questions you need to answer. First, did you have permission from a responsible consultant to carry out this experiment?'

'No,' said Stephen, after searching vainly for a way out.

'Secondly, did you apply to this ethical committee to carry out this experiment?'

Again Stephen agreed he had not.

'Thirdly, do you not agree that you had no idea what would happen when you meddled with this young lady's psychological health, and as a consequence put her in grave danger?'

Stephen now had a chance to turn this inquisition round. 'In answering this, I would like to take a broader look at the Poleaxe Syndrome. Despite many theories, nobody has a clear idea as to its cause. It may be an infection, it may be a neurological disorder, it may be an inflammatory condition, but as we do not know, we have no idea if our well-meaning interventions are doing good or harm.'

Leonard was not going to let him explain. 'We are not here to discuss the origins of Poleaxe. Please confine your answers to the matter in hand.'

'This is the matter in hand. We want new insight into this condition and my investigations suggest that the mental states of the people who get the Poleaxe Syndrome have a common feature, a foreboding sense of anxiety and dissolution, and it is this that leads to collapse and temporary paralysis of the limbs.'

It was not working. Leonard had heard enough. 'We are not here to listen to your theories. Do you not agree that you meddled with the health of this young woman in an experiment that was not approved by any authority at this hospital?'

Stephen was expecting criticisms of the word 'experiment'. It gave the impression that he was a hard, unfeeling scientist who would put people through suffering just to vindicate his theories. So he had prepared his response. 'I agree it was not approved, but when a doctor tries a new approach with a patient it does not necessarily require formal approval, especially with a very serious condition like Poleaxe that needs all forms of enquiry urgently. When Joseph Lister revolutionised surgery by using antiseptic techniques and phenol spray when operating on an eleven-year-old boy in Glasgow in 1865, he did not go to an ethical committee to get approval.'

Leonard was now exasperated. 'But that was a hundred years ago; we are now in 1967 and are more aware of risk. In any case, Joseph Lister was a qualified surgeon; you, as a junior doctor in mental health, have no business coming into a general hospital and peddling your odd ideas.'

Stephen decided he had to defend his profession. He was not going to give in to this bully. 'The knife of disease does not respect professional boundaries; it cuts through them. I put it to you that every patient in this hospital has a mental health component to their condition, and it is right and proper that we, with special knowledge in mental health, have a part to play in understanding and helping them.'

Leonard had to let others take part. Stephen felt he was losing his grip.

'I am sure my other colleagues have questions too.'

Peggy had to buttress her master inquisitor. 'You said you had the agreement of Miss BD to take part in your experiment. Did you obtain this in writing, and, if not, why not?'

'I obtained verbal consent. As the patient is still on the ward, you can ask her yourself if you wish.'

'That is not the point. All new experimental procedures have to be approved in writing.'

Stephen suspected that bureaucracy was winning here.

But then Christopher Barclay intervened. 'Could I ask you what led to your hypothesis? I see many patients who have what I call "hysterical hypochondriasis", as they are mentally unwell but express all their symptoms in physical form. Are you suggesting that the Poleaxe Syndrome is similar to these conditions?'

At last, a sensible question for Stephen to answer without being interrupted. 'No, it is not the same. Poleaxe clearly is a physical disease associated with unequivocal signs and can be fatal. But what I suspect is that only some people get the disease because of their mental predispositions. To be absolutely honest, the first person to propose this idea was the patient, Miss BD. To put her into context, her name is Barbara Dukinfield, and she noted that all her fellow sufferers with the Poleaxe Syndrome were highly anxious people. She passed this on to Dr Camberwell and also to me.'

Leonard interrupted. 'You have broken the patient's confidence by mentioning her name. Could I ask all the members of this committee to erase this name from their minds. It will also not appear in the record of this meeting. I think you have said enough, Dr Bollider, and before you get yourself into deeper water, I would like you to leave the meeting and wait outside until we call you.'

Stephen dutifully rose and went outside. He sat on an uncomfortable wicker chair by the entrance, feeling equally uncomfortable inside. He did not have a bevy of support in the meeting, but he could not have done much better. He was not going to be bowed down.

After a few minutes, which seemed like an hour, Stephen was called back in.

Leonard stared at him closely. 'Dr Bollider, we have discussed your case and will be making a report that will be sent to your superiors and included in our official communications. You have been found to have broken our ethical guidelines in seeing a patient under the care of this hospital, treating them without adequate consent or oversight, and putting the patient at risk. As a consequence, you will not be allowed back into this hospital without supervision from a senior colleague at this hospital. As this is a first offence, we have decided not to report you to the General Medical Council, but this breach will be noted in your records.'

Stephen was stunned but not contrite.

'Have you anything to say, Dr Bollider?'

'Only that I have always tried to follow the Hippocratic oath that all doctors should follow but sometimes forget, that in any hospital or home "I will enter to help the sick and abstain from all wrong-doing". I do not feel I have broken that oath by any of my actions and that all doctors have an equal right to enter hospitals and do their best for the sick.'

'You are prevaricating again. Do you wish to make an apology to this committee for your behaviour?'

Stephen had been able to contain his emotions until now, but this silly man was insufferable. 'No, apart from saying I am sorry that you, especially you, Dr Nolan, have failed to listen to my arguments. I believe I have behaved ethically and properly in my work, and you will shortly be reading about it in the journals. You cannot suppress science.'

Stephen sounded more pompous than he intended but felt he must have the last word in this kangaroo court, so, without waiting, he turned and left this room of fractious and unnecessary interrogation.

TWENTY-TWO

DAY SIXTY-SEVEN, ONE NEW CASE, NO NEW DEATHS

Speak of me as I am,
Nothing extenuate

William Shakespeare, *Othello*, 1604

Barbara climbed out the bath and stood in front of the mirror, warm and steaming. She liked to have her baths hot. She had asked the ward staff to allow her to have this in mid-afternoon, when she knew all would be quiet and she could wallow in the warmth.

She looked critically at her reflection, only partly blurred by steam.

'So there you are, Barbara Dukinfield. What have you got to say for yourself?'

She surveyed her body. Yes, she was conventionally pretty, but there was nothing distinctive about her. No flaming hair, no aquiline nose, no seductive mouth. Instead, an oval to roundish face, light brown hair, lips that she liked to think were full, but were not quite, and which were upturned at the corners, making her look as though she had a permanent smile. This was not an advantage, and 'What are you smirking at, Dukinfield?' had become a frequent unnecessary question. Further down, good figure, passable waist, reasonable-sized firm breasts, but she would have liked them a bit fuller, and good legs. Yes, she liked her legs. They were just right in shape and length.

But overall, not much to really like, no distinctive features. And she could not understand why older women were so bothered about lines. If only she could have a line or two; it would give her bland face character.

She stepped back a little to see her full body in the mirror.

'Let's face it, Dukinfield. You're ordinary.'

But what about the rest of her, the more important part that was not just skin-deep? She had become aware of her own mortality with the deaths on the ward, especially poor Fred Entwistle, whom she had grown to like so much. The memory of him dying suddenly, right next to her, with no apparent warning, was a searing one. She could easily have died too. This Poleaxe did not discriminate between people. And here she was, nineteen years old, a quarter of the way through her life, and what had she achieved?

And if she had died instead of Fred, what would be her obituary? Of course, she would not have a published one, only a little paragraph in the church magazine. She imagined what her parents would write first:

Barbara Dukinfield
God-fearing
The sweetest of daughters
Always helpful and caring
Never a harsh word
Lovely disposition
Very sadly missed

But of course this would only be an accurate reflection for them and their friends. Her innermost irritations, impulses and insubordination were never expressed. She was convinced she was quite a nasty person underneath, but always managed to suppress her emotions except when her mother drove her to the limits of her tolerance.

So what would God have written on the mirror? She felt God was on her side. He had to be, as in her view many of the congregation at her father's church were not exactly his ardent followers, and she needed to believe in more. Barbara was determined to be generous in her opinion of others. This was the Christian way, but had she been too understanding? Yet the small-minded meanness, so rife in the church, troubled her faith. This was where the place where it should not have been expected. Too many were so preoccupied with booking their place in heaven, they had forgotten they were still travelling on earth.

So God was all-seeing and all-knowing. What would He have written, provided He had time to spare from all his other activities? She decided to write them down with her finger in the steam of the bathroom mirror. God, of course, would know them already, but she needed a reminder for herself.

Tried to be God-fearing
Was kind and generous to others
Mother-dominated
Scraped into university
A virgin

She looked at what she had written again as she started to dry herself with one of the very large bath towels they provided at Medenby Hospital.

Yes, God had it right. She was God-fearing, but this was partly a consequence of her natural anxiety, although she was pleased this was beginning to lessen. Fear was not a desirable emotion. She would much prefer to become God-embracing in time.

'Was kind and generous to others'. Yes, that was completely accurate. It was her good point. Every time she said or did anything she thought about it beforehand, and, if there was any possibility of creating offence, she would suppress the thought, action or word. Mrs Cadwallader, round the corner from the Manse, was an impossible woman who spent all her time complaining to her father about the church. It was her hobby. There was nothing that she would not complain about. She even complained to her father that she had to take up the mantle of complaint as nobody else would take it on. But Barbara had gone out of her way to be exceptionally attentive and nice to her. This was where she was generous; she made the most effort to those who were the most self-centred and, in her opinion, lacked a proper soul. She felt sometimes she could inject soul into people who had never felt it before, as very occasionally she had helped people to change. But when it failed, she felt like a pompous little do-gooding madam, interfering unnecessarily in other's lives.

Mother-dominated. God would have to agree here. Pamela Dukinfield was a good mother, but she regarded her daughter as an extension of herself. Left to her own designs as a child, and often lost, she was determined that her daughter would have a better upbringing. She would be taught and tutored well, and would never be ignored. But this, of course, was no way to bring up her daughter.

Barbara was praised for being diligent, obedient and acquiescent, but never allowed to be independent. The most important thing Pamela Dukinfield wanted to avoid was the possibility of her daughter 'going off the rails'. She was not quite sure how leaving the rails might be manifest but had the notion it could be prevented if good mothers could always be there to love, advise and control.

As a consequence, Barbara had now become resentful, cautious and inhibited at home. She was reminded over and over again that she must love her mother in return for all the affection and concern that she had received. But love had been steadily leached from her constitution over the years so now she sometimes felt, quite unfairly, that Pamela was a hateful figure, not a beneficent one.

As for scraping into university, this was more an attempt to get away from home rather than to pursue an academic calling, but Barbara had to admit that her choice of anthropology was a good one. She liked her course, loved jousting with her fellow students, and could not wait to leave home and live in college for her second year.

She looked again at the list on the steamed mirror, now looking less legible as the steam condensed and the words dribbled down, obscuring those below.

A virgin. The words were getting blurred. 'Aversion' was the word replacing it. Was there a message there? Now, would God be pleased she was a virgin? When she looked at all the words on the mirror she could not help noticing that all her reported assets were attributes given to, or promoted by, her parents, with the possible exception of generosity. What had she done that was entirely her decision alone?

Being a virgin was the only one. She had decided, early on, that she would save herself for the right man. She had a higher view of sex. It was not something to be casually set aside. It was special, and no matter now often girls at school had talked about it as a badge of esteem or a sign of maturity, using language that she simply found offensive, she kept it special in her mind.

But this was something that was under her control. Neither Pamela nor Robert Dukinfield had anything to do with it. So it could be changed easily by her actions alone.

So she tried an experiment. She liked the word 'experiment', introduced in its proper sense to her by Stephen. Testing something, then seeing if it worked. Underneath the last word on the bathroom mirror she wrote:

Never been f****d

She could not allow herself to spell out the last word, as she had always found it extremely rude, but there was no other way of putting it.

Would God be pleased that she was a virgin, and would He be offended by adding the extra three words to her list? Were these three words a better description than 'a virgin'? She thought for a short time and decided that he would not be offended at all. One was a passive state, almost implying persistence, the second expression described something that had not yet happened but might be expected to at some time. It had much more meaning. God would expect a girl like her to be f****d at some time, unless she was destined to become a nun, and that was the last thing on Barbara's mind.

God would not be offended by words that were completely accurate. He had given her a reasonable body, an acceptable brain and a positive attitude to life and sex, and he would actually want her to be f****d. If virginity was preventing her from making progress in her life, it should be tossed aside.

And she had to look ahead. She wanted to have sex; she wanted to be a mother. Motherhood was on another planet, but she knew she must travel to it eventually. To be a mother, to hold babies that had come from her own body, must be her aim and, eventually, her most successful achievement. Most of all, she yearned to be fertile. And she would have at least two children. An only child always had to be acutely aware of their parents; two children need only to be aware of each other and could ignore their parents at times. How often had she intoned, 'Oh, how I wish Mum and Dad could have realised I needed a brother or a sister. I hope I wasn't the reason why they had no more.'

But before all these anticipated developments she had to lose her virginity. What a silly expression that was. She had no wish to lose anything. There was everything to gain. But how would she go about this? It was clear, abundantly clear, that a lot of people wanted to have sex with her. Fending them off over the years had become quite an art.

This was indeed a serious problem. She could not talk about it freely with anyone. Fortunately, or perhaps unfortunately in retrospect, at the age of fifteen she had picked up a book from the public library that helped her enormously. It was by a well-known author, Kingsley Amis, and called *Take a Girl Like You*. Barbara was not a great reader, but this book, almost picked up at random when she was scanning the titles, was spot on. She identified immediately with the main character, Jenny Bunn, a girl of twenty who throughout the book was harassed to lose her virginity by a host of creepy men. 'Jenny Bunn is me, how did he know?' asked the fifteen-year-old Barbara incredulously, and she followed much of the advice coming from Jenny's experiences. She renewed the book three times at the library and carried it permanently in her school satchel – her mother must never be allowed to see it.

One of the most important messages was to avoid 'horizontal love-making'. This was dangerous to good virgins, as in this position they were much more vulnerable. But this Kingsley Amis wrote about it all as though it was a great joke; to the young Barbara it was deadly serious. So the teenage Barbara had made sure than she was never in dark places with a man on his own, particularly when surrounded by couches, beds or even plush carpets.

But the book had a sad ending. Jenny Bunn lost her virginity in an alcoholic haze and knew nothing about it. Barbara was determined that, whatever else happened, she would lose her virginity when she was fully conscious and completely aware. She wanted an experience to remember.

But had it been helpful to travel on this journey of virtuous chastity? She could not agree that it had, however much she wanted to. Now she was nineteen she still knew nothing significant about men, had rarely had a sensible conversation with a boy of her own age as she was so good at avoiding them, and was still a virgin.

That was why it had been so refreshing talking to Stephen. He treated her as an equal, listened carefully to her opinions and praised her without being slimy. And she had the feeling he was fond of her. When she was with him he spent a lot of the time looking at her, and his gaze did not appear to be dominated by science. And when she had hugged him after the successful experiment – she still did not know what made her do it – he was rather slow to let go.

There was a knock on the bathroom door.

'Have you finished, Barbara? I hope you can be out in the next five minutes, as there is a queue building up.'

'Of course, Nurse Fordham. Sorry to be a slow coach.'

She rubbed off the words on the steamy mirror, all except the bottom three. They had to be changed.

Never been fucked

She'd finally done it, written the letters of the word she had been avoiding all her life. Goodbye all those castrated verbs and nouns like 'copulation', 'carnal knowledge', 'sexual intercourse' and 'consummation', and the words preceding 'with' that puzzled her so much as a child: 'go', 'sleep', 'be intimate', 'going to bed'. Welcome to the word that described what she wanted and needed.

She gave the words one last look before removing them with her towel. Now she must have a plan. Whatever else happened in her life, she was not going to die a virgin.

TWENTY-THREE

DAY SIXTY-NINE, ONE NEW CASE, NO NEW DEATHS

*A king is always a king – and a woman
always a woman; his authority and her sex
ever stand between them and rational converse*

Mary Shelley, 1831

Stephen had arranged to see Barbara at the back of the large car park at Medenby Hospital. He had been banned from going to the ward again after the meeting of the Ethics Committee, but Barbara had to give him some more questionnaires she had completed by the other patients recovering from Poleaxe. Giles, who had been shocked by the way Stephen had been treated by the Ethics Committee, was only too pleased to help to fix up the visit. Barbara was now allowed to leave the ward for short periods and so was able to meet him at the planned time.

The car park was empty. It was an overspill one and Stephen was pleased they would not be disturbed. He stopped the car under the shade of a large oak tree and waited. Good, he could see her enter, a hundred yards away. As she approached he could appreciate her appearance properly for the first time. She was wearing a simple dress with a cord round the waist, accentuating her firm high breasts and slim figure. As she got closer he could see the inviting red and white floral pattern of the dress clinging to her body. It did not matter that she was not wearing make-up. It was completely unnecessary.

He opened the passenger car door to let her in. She put the papers in the glove compartment and then, without a word, lay down on his lap and looked up at him. He did not respond, not sure what to do.

'Take me, Stephen.'

'I'm not sure what you mean. Take you, where to?'

'Don't be silly – you know what I mean.' She pulled his face down towards her own.

Stephen was flabbergasted. He liked to predict what might happen during the course of the average day, but this was completely outside his range. 'I'm not sure if I fully understand you, Barbara. Have you really thought this through?'

She looked at him quizzically. Had she really thought it through? There seemed an element of doubt. Was she in familiar territory? They both looked at each other, slightly askance, both waiting for the next move.

Stephen broke the silence. 'We, as doctors, are advised, very strongly, not to have intimate relations with our patients, as it might be considered to be exploitation.'

Barbara laughed. 'Come off it, Stephen. You are not my doctor. You come from another hospital. You're a friend. You can be as intimate as you like with me.'

'But you hardly know me. And do you know I am married?'

'I guessed you might be, Stephen.' She looked at him again. 'Sorry to put you in a dilemma.'

Stephen resolved this dilemma by kissing her, gently rather than passionately, and looking carefully at her eyes for clues. Was she really infatuated with him or was her attraction towards him something to do with Poleaxe? Was heightened sexual interest a consequence of the disease? He could not stop scientific analysis even in a situation like this.

'Have you done this sort of thing before?'

'Of course I have.' Barbara pulled him down towards her again and kissed him, long and deep, exploring every crevice in his mouth with her tongue.

But Stephen remained unconvinced. He was sure she was not a femme fatale. 'I don't believe you, Barbara. I think you're experimenting.' Stephen was sure if she was or not, but he could not help feeling he was part of an experiment that he might have started unwittingly by his hypnosis.

Barbara was nonplussed. 'Experimenting, really? Is sex an experiment?'

Stephen pounced on this. 'Ah, by saying that, I bet you are telling me you are not sexually experienced. Have I got it right?'

Barbara sniffed. 'I suppose you have.'

'So why the change?'

'After you carried out that experiment over two weeks ago, I felt liberated. Not just because it seemed to explain Poleaxe, but it also freed me up to be what I am. I realised I was a proper functioning woman. You gave me confidence, otherwise I wouldn't be lying on your lap now, talking like this. And I want to convince you that my proposition is right for me and not just a sudden fancy.'

'I still can't get my head around this. You've been a great help to me and I know we can work together, but this takes everything to a new plane.'

She laughed but said nothing and just looked at him. It was a curious hiatus. She had come with one thought in her mind and it had become diverted. Now they were discussing her feelings as though they were an extension of their earlier discussions in hospital. Stephen, a logical thinker, was happier in this mode. But Barbara was determined to change course. She pulled up her dress and exposed her velvety body, free of bra and knickers. She had come prepared. Her breasts lay open before him: round, inviting and with nipples perched erect. She looked at him again.

Now desire was beginning to take over from logic, but Stephen was determined to hang on a little longer. 'I just can't make up my mind.'

'Can I help you, Stephen? I'm an anthropologist, and know how different societies work. What do you think everybody in these societies enjoy doing most of all?'

She reached up to kiss him again, but he suddenly pulled away.

'But I haven't got a condom.'

'Oh no. I thought all doctors had a supply of condoms handy.'

'Of course not. I don't make a practice of regular sex in my car. I'm not a Don Juan, just a jobbing psychiatrist, and just in case you don't know, we don't spend all our time talking about sex, or even practising it.'

Barbara gave him another kiss, not so passionate this time. She pulled her dress down over her knees and sat demurely in the passenger seat again. 'Sorry, the seductress didn't think of everything. But I've an idea.'

She looked in her bag and took out a notebook and a diary. She looked at the diary, tore a page from the book and wrote '28th June, Shirewood Forest Car Park, 10.30pm'. 'I hope you can make this date. I'll be out of hospital by then and we can meet in the evening. That's a much more romantic place than your car.'

Stephen could hardly keep up with this enchantress of sex. All he could do is to kiss her again, powerfully and intensely, showing that whatever she wanted was reciprocated, but he had to overcome all his doubts first. But he had to stop kissing her before he went too far. He was getting dangerously close.

'You must get back to the ward.'

'Yes, I will, Stephen.' She opened the door. 'And please remember, nobody else is going to know about this. Absolutely nobody. I'm good at keeping secrets, and hope you can keep mine.'

She blew him a kiss as she turned from the car, swinging her hips and striding confidently away. It was clear she at any rate had no doubts about what she had done. Stephen could not stop looking at her until she had completely disappeared from view.

And of course she was right. She wanted him to take part in an experiment, a pretty straightforward one. It probably had nothing to do with Poleaxe. But it was still very strange. Temptation was a motley blessing.

TWENTY-FOUR

DAY SEVENTY-ONE, ONE NEW CASE

*If I really seem vain, it is that I am only vain in my ways –
not in my heart*

Thomas Hardy, 1873

'I am glad to say that we have now turned the corner. After days of increasing cases of Poleaxe, things have settled. We are now on top of the disease. We will continue to give bulletins about Poleaxe, but instead of giving you the total number of cases we will now only give the number of new cases each day, and sadly, any deaths when they occur. We are hopeful that both will stay close to zero.'

James finished his Radio Medenby Poleaxe report.

'Great stuff, James,' said the DJ on the desk. 'You've really socked it to them, and we're now the most popular local radio in the country.'

'I have to thank you for allowing me to keep everyone informed so comprehensively.' James must not allow elation to prevent honourable modesty.

147

'We were only doing our bit. This is what local radio is for. Everyone knowing what is happening when it is happening. Until we can get telephones that can do the same job, we're going to be in business.'

James walked outside Radio Medenby's cramped little office in the corner of the grounds of the primary school and unlocked his car. Radio Medenby needed a leg up in the world and he was pleased to have been able to provide it. All in all, it had been a most satisfying day. Everything was falling into place and he was no longer a spectator.

He arrived home early. There was nothing more to do in the office and Poleaxe had suppressed all other tasks in the public health department. Elaine was at home and could see he was triumphant.

'Good day – don't tell me.'

James gave her a powerful kiss. He was bubbling with happiness. Elaine was impressed. This was the man she had married. An idealist, with strong views about equity and opportunity, with uplifting aspirations about improving society, but until the Poleaxe problem had appeared he seemed to be embittered and discontented. Others were always standing in his way. Now things had changed. He had recovered his zeal.

James could only talk frankly to Elaine. He did not trust anybody else. 'They have to take notice of me now. Closing off Medenby was the master stroke. It's worked. We now have no new cases outside Medenby, and I am rightly getting the credit. I've just had a meeting of the Poleaxe Task Group. They could not stop complimenting me – even though I thought some were rather more forced than spontaneous. This is going to turn out very well for us. Possibly an appointment as MOH at Manchester or Leeds, or at the very least an OBE.'

'Now that's a change of mind for you. You always used to say that stood for "Other Buggers' Efforts".'

'Yes, but on this occasion this particular bugger did it on his own.'

'Absolutely. And you know what? I guessed this would be a good day and have booked a table for dinner at the Beckingham Arms by the river this evening. And afterwards, if you're interested, I'll allow you to ravage me. I've been reading *Venus and Adonis* this afternoon, so I'm in the mood. Graze on my lips, and if those hills be dry, stray lower, where the pleasant fountains lie.'

Elaine leant over James with her blouse undone, showing a glimpse of her pleasant fountains.

James was aroused. 'That sounds to be a marvellous idea. Old-fashioned eating and ravaging make a most satisfying menu. I will harness all my primitive urges in preparation. But perhaps I will start gently with a beer.'

'Of course, darling. Pop next door and I'll get it for you.'

James went through and sat in his favourite armchair by the fire. Elaine brought him his tankard of beer. This was certainly going to be a day to savour. As his lips dipped through the foaming head to the cool, rewarding hop-ladened liquor beneath, he breathed a large sigh of relief. It had been a strain at times, but the rewards had come. What else could this day bring?

As he thought about the evening, and the night that would follow, there was a scratching noise at the back of his chair. Of course, there was another chapter to savour in the book of the day – the Snow Dance.

He waited for the next stage in what had now become an evening ritual. The scratching was just the beginning of the performance, the slow-motion bolero dance of the evening. A few seconds later Snow jumped up to the top of the chair, placed his paws on James's head, moved his head languidly from side to side and then thrust his front paws into his thick black hair. After a gentle paw massage, he sat back on the chair before jumping down to the arm. The next movement was the downsweep of his long body to James's lap, where he continued his twisting, sinuous dance for another twenty seconds or so. He then turned and looked at James for the first time in this dance routine. After a long stare, he comforted himself by lying down on James's chest and opening his mouth in a very large yawn. The final movement of the bolero was completed by Snow placing his front paws on James's chest just below his top shirt button. This was the perfect ending; the rendition of a small tiger settled and proud on top of his prey.

James knew all the movements and appreciated he was the passive partner in this ritual. But that was the good thing about cats. They did not praise or flatter, they did not need to impress, they followed their routines in their own way and in their own time, and yet retained an endearing element of loyalty that was never cloying or demanding. Yes, he needed Snow to keep him on the level.

TWENTY-FIVE

DAY SEVENTY-TWO, NO NEW CASES

*From this moment I began to conclude in my mind that it
was possible for me to be more happy in this forsaken, solitary
condition that it was possible I should ever have been in any
other particular state in the world*

Daniel Defoe, 1719

James had left the latest Poleaxe meeting feeling supremely
pleased. Everything was indeed going his way. He had
been praised for his energy and commitment, thanked
for his perseverance and even congratulated by William
Fothergill, who rarely had a positive word for anybody.
Who could ask for more?

He would not go home immediately; he fancied a beer.
A good pint in the Prince Henry would be his own minor
self-reward. As he walked along the London Road, he was
impressed by the number of people on the narrow streets
in the centre of town. The fear of Poleaxe was diminishing
and confidence was returning. Excellent.

As he turned into Storeman Street the crowds became larger. He was recognised.

'There's Dr Porton. He's the hero of Medenby,' shouted someone. 'Let's show him.'

James, not exactly sure what was being shown, was then propelled by the crowd into the Prince Henry, a faded, half-timbered public house showing its advanced age, but still proudly reminding all that it had survived the Civil War when Medenby was besieged. Squashed between the more recent buildings, it was squeezed, distorted and rickety, but there was something about the bright sign outside that informed the world that it would outlive its upstart neighbours on either side.

The crowd in the pub also cheered as he came in. 'Well done, Jimmy, mate. Get him a beer,' shouted a man at the bar, his moustache and beard speckled white with froth.

'What on earth...' protested James, pleased and uplifted by all the smiling faces.

The bearded young man continued, 'You've given us back our town. Nobody cared about Medenby before you came along. You're the one who's put us on the map. Now we are the news: not London, not Nottingham, not Leicester. We're now a favoured island in the sea of England. All famous – thanks to you.'

'But I haven't done anything, just trying to sort out the Poleaxe problem.'

'That's where you're wrong, Jim boy. People don't tune into national radio now; they listen to Radio Medenby and your broadcasts. You tell them how we're standing up to this disease, how we're fighting it, how we deal with these roadblocks and all, and how tough we all are.'

'Quite right,' shouted an older, balder man, waving a beer mug unsteadily, 'my sister keeps phoning me to cheer me up. She thinks I'm really suffering, and I haven't the heart to tell her I'm having the time of my life. I've never felt so important. Everyone wants me now. Before you and Poleaxe came along, no-one cared a sausage.'

James was invigorated, but as he picked up his proffered beer, he felt he must try and return to his serious role as Medical Officer of Health. 'But you've had a difficult time. Not being able to leave the town without permission, having to eat differently, even having to pay more for your beer. Why does that help?'

'They're nothing. It's just that we in Medenby have now got things under our control,' said the balding man, splashing his beer on the bar top. 'We know what we have to do. We don't need to depend on others, so we work things out for ourselves. Poleaxe isn't nice to have in our town, but it's made us come together. We all look out for each other now; we really do. It wasn't the same before.'

'It's very good to hear that. But we're getting the disease under control now, so how will you feel when it's all over? When Poleaxe has gone, will you be disappointed?'

There was a chorus of disapproval. 'Not at all,' said a small, neat man whom James recognised as an assistant in the library. 'You've given us back our self-respect. When we were a major market town, we were properly treated. But we've slipped back recently. What you've done, without any of us properly knowing it, is to give us our self-respect back. We are now the tough, unflinching and unabashed people of Medenby, able to face the world with a smile and resolve we never thought we had.'

This was getting a little too complicated for the pub regulars. 'Tell that to Medenby Town Football Club – they could do with a bit of that for next season,' shouted one.

There were yet more cheers, and such was the infectious enthusiasm of the moment that this normally quiet group of citizens were compelled to break into song. So it was, that on this muggy evening June day, that the raucous sounds of 'he's a jolly good fellow', ending in its crescendo of 'and so say all of us', were heard with quiet bemusement by the people walking towards the Market Square from the narrows of Storeman Street. What they were celebrating they could not guess, but it was good that some had cause to cheer.

James left the Prince Henry when the fuss had died down. As he drove home he reflected on how far he had come since that first meeting with William Fothergill. He had taken the Poleaxe tide at the flood and brought it to fame and fortune. Did he deserve all the adulation he was now receiving? Possibly not, but he could not help feeling important for the first time in his life. All the other occasions, from the time he first got his scholarship to the grammar school, were times when he was the projection of other people's achievements, not his own; creating plaudits for his parents, his school, his debating society. At these occasions he felt like a puppet, dangled in front of people while others operated the strings. 'Look at James, look how well he's done, haven't we done well too, as he is a product of our work.'

Now he was being important in his own right, and it felt good. He was not triumphant about it; he was just extraordinarily satisfied. Not smug as some might think, just that for the first time in his life the person he had always wanted to be was here inside his skin. There was no need to go on striving to get to a higher plane, as he was already on it. And it did not matter that some people, like the crowds at Medenby, were praising him inappropriately. He had made a positive difference to the world, and nobody could take it away from him. And Medenby, a favoured island in the sea of England, that was a lovely touch.

Elaine was waiting for him when he arrived home. 'Just in time, darling. Dinner's almost ready and the cat's been fed. How did it all go?'

He kissed her quickly on the forehead while she was cooking. 'I think we've won the battle. Everyone agrees the disease is now contained, and there is no doubt it's an infectious one. I'm very popular in the town now. They've literally been singing my praises at the Prince Henry.'

'That's marvellous – and well deserved. Now sit yourself down next door and I'll bring you your sherry.'

James loosened his tie and slumped into his favourite chair. Snow was waiting and carried out his evening ritual before jumping up and placing his paws firmly on his chest. He had to ask him a question. Snow would know the answer.

'Am I not the most important person in Medenby now?'

Snow stared intently, his green eyes looking straight through him. 'No, you are not. I am.'

'But we have saved the country from Poleaxe. Does not that make me more important than you?'

'Do not get above your station, Dr Porton. Self-promotion only reflects insecurity. Look into my eyes for certainty to be seen.'

Elaine came in with the sherry. 'Yes, I knew it. Snow's on your lap again. He's been waiting for you all day. Seems to have been worried today, for some reason, but he'll be all right now.'

James agreed. He would be too.

TWENTY-SIX

DAY SEVENTY-FOUR, NO NEW CASES

*It is the responsibility of the media to look at the President
with a microscope, but they go too far when they use a
proctoscope.*

Richard Nixon, 1974

James arrived early at the BBC's Lime Grove studios in
West London. He walked past the drab Victorian houses
in the street off Wood Lane towards the converted building
looking more like a warehouse than a television studio.
This surprised but rather pleased him, for he believed that
a public service did not need ostentation. The studio's
ordinariness made him feel more at home. He was to be
interviewed by David Frost, a young man who had made
quite a name for himself as a television presenter, and who
some described as a man made for the camera, whatever
that meant.

He entered, confirmed his credentials to an officious
clerk who would have looked more at home in a police

station, and was escorted upstairs to the studio, where he was attended to by a make-up artist.

'We're just going to lighten up your features,' the young blonde whispered. 'We don't want you looking grey. David will see you in the main studio when he's ready.'

As he waited, James rehearsed his lines. This should be relatively easy. The interview would be short. All he had to do was to reassure the viewers that the epidemic was under control and that they were close to finding its cause. No empty words, just straightforward facts. But his mouth was dry. Why was this such an ordeal?

The door opened and he was beckoned in. There was David, looking smarter than James expected, wearing a dark grey suit and waistcoat, white shirt with a cut-back collar. He gave a welcoming smile that James interpreted as neutral rather than friendly. The cameras were ready.

'Good afternoon, hello, and welcome. We are pleased to meet Dr James Porton, Medical Officer of Health for Medenby, who will be talking about the mysterious syndrome, Poleaxe, that has affected many in the town, some, very sadly, with fatal consequences. Dr Porton, can you bring us up to date?'

James was ready and bursting to go. 'I think the important message is that the Poleaxe Syndrome is now under control. We know it is an infection and are close to identifying its nature and its source. Since we sealed off the town of Medenby to prevent further spread of the disease, we have only had one new case. So our efforts now are focused on identifying the exact nature of the infectious agent.' He sat back, pleased.

David, however, leant forward. 'Thank you, that is very helpful, and encouraging. But I understand that there is still some doubt about the nature of the disease and its cause.'

'I'm not exactly sure what you mean.'

David leant sideways to pick up a copy of the *British Medical Journal*. He stared at James. 'One of your colleagues in Medenby has just written this letter in the *British Medical Journal*. I'm sure you must have seen it, but I will read the important section for the viewers.' He read in a firm, clear voice: 'I conclude that anxiety is an important component of the Poleaxe Syndrome and is a potential cause rather than a consequence of the disease. This requires further investigation.'

He looked again at James and pointed a finger at him, an action that James perceived as aggressive. 'I am not a medical man, but doesn't this seem to suggest you have quite a long way to go before you can be confident about the cause?'

James thought he detected a sneer behind the question and felt one or two hackles rise. He was half expecting this, and of course he had read the article. He had a response ready and had to express it firmly. 'Of course any disease like this makes people anxious. What is so surprising about that? I am sure, Mr Frost, when you have been unwell that you too have been anxious.' James wanted to go on the offensive here. He was sure he was in safe territory.

'We are to discuss Poleaxe, not my niggling complaints. Newsworthy they are not; boring, yes.' David beamed at the camera. 'The point your colleague is making, Dr Porton, is that anxiety is present before people develop Poleaxe. Perhaps it is not just a consequence, but a cause.'

James was irritated. A hot kernel of temper rose inside him. 'I want to stress that the person who has made these suggestions is not a colleague of mine. He is a junior doctor in a local mental hospital and has no understanding of the complexity of physical disease.'

David looked quizzically at James. 'But it looks as though he has presented a strong case. Are you suggesting that he is misguided, or may even be a charlatan?'

James's temper took over. He plunged into its maelstrom. 'I don't know his intentions. What I do know is that he is unfairly stigmatising the victims of this unfortunate syndrome by claiming they are just anxious. They are not. They have been through a terrible ordeal and some have died. They have suffered enough without people who know nothing about proper medicine interfering in their care.'

'So what advice would you give now?'

'It's very simple. Stay out of subjects you do not understand and leave it to the experts. Doctors who work in mental hospitals understand mental patients – at least I hope so – but they should not interfere with the work of others. It's not their territory.'

James thought he had closed the discussion, but David was not finished. Leaning forward again, looking puzzled, he continued, 'I am sorry if I appear to be obtuse, but are you saying that there is no place for mental health professionals in general hospitals? Could it not be that many people in all kinds of hospitals, not just mental ones, have emotional and other problems and that appropriately trained staff should deal with these?'

James was all wound up. All his frustrations with Stephen Bollider spilled over. 'That's different. The doctor to whom you are referring went into our hospital without being invited, carried out experiments without approval on sick patients, and then had the impudence to write about his results without any proper supervision. This is a disgrace and is currently being addressed by our medical authorities. He may no longer be allowed to practise.'

David seemed to be relishing this interview. He had not finished. 'Do I take it, Dr Porton, that you do not think highly of those who practise the treatment of mental illness? Is not that view becoming a little old-fashioned now that we are getting more aware of its importance in medicine?'

James understood he was being provoked but could not resist the bait. 'You have to understand, Mr Frost, that the reason why psychiatrists practise in mental hospitals is because they and their patients belong there, not in general hospitals. To suggest that they should be gadding about drumming up trade, as it were, by seeing everybody who might have a bit of mental distress here or some funny worries there, is ludicrous. I am surprised that a man of your intelligence even contemplates this.' James realised the noise he made in finishing this response was the stamping of his right foot. Good, let this reinforce the point.

David smiled at the camera beatifically. 'Thank you, Dr Porton, for a most elucidating interview. I think all our viewers will understand the Poleaxe Syndrome better now.'

James walked out into the late afternoon heat of the day. He needed air, and time to think. He could not remember clearly all of what he had said but had the feeling he had not been in full control. But at another level he felt relieved and vindicated. He had got something important off his chest, and it may not have been completely wise to share this with a million television viewers, but he was sure they would support his views. His job was not just to find the cause of the disease, but to remove the stain of pop psychology from an illness that had no right to be contaminated.

TWENTY-SEVEN

DAY SEVENTY-SIX, NO NEW CASES

The power to label is the power to destroy

Allen Frances, 2013

Stephen's day had been interrupted by frequent telephone calls from reporters. They were all asking about Poleaxe, trying to add to the recent headlines in the national papers. He shuddered. 'Poleaxe Victims Bonkers, Claims Mind Doc', shouted *The Sun*. 'Curious challenge to Poleaxe diagnosis', ventured *The Times*. 'Not the whole facts, says doctor about Poleaxe', quipped the *Daily Mail*. *The Guardian* kept it sober but obscure: 'Disease origin questioned', was the header of a small column on page two. Only *The Daily Telegraph* got close to the nub with its headline: 'Anxiety rather than infection: new Poleaxe theory?'

The journalists' questions had been predictable. Silly, aggressive, loaded. 'Why do you think the other doctors have got it wrong?' 'Do you think Poleaxe is all in the mind?' 'Would you say those who have died were just scared to death?' Questions that were designed to catch him out, to make him say something stupid. After a little, he gave up trying to answer and just referred them to his letter in the *BMJ*.

He could not help thinking how different if he, rather than being a psychiatrist, was just another doctor piecing the Poleaxe Syndrome together with others. By tossing a mental health component into the fray, he was viewed as a wrecker, not a builder of evidence. After these phone interruptions it was quite a relief to be just doing his normal job. He was on call and in the evening there were two emergency admissions to assess, arrange initial care for and settle for the night. One of these patients clearly had bipolar disorder and, in the heightened awareness of his manic state, had picked up from the phone calls a hint of what was going on. Manic patients had a nose for detection beyond that of other mortals, even if they sometimes missed the gist.

'You tell them, Doc. They're just a bunch of old hacks running after polecats; catch them in the trees, hit 'em when they sneeze.'

'Flight of ideas with rhyming slang' wrote Stephen in the medical notes as he confirmed the diagnosis of 'bipolar disorder – hypomanic phase'. He prescribed an antipsychotic and a sedative, before writing in the notes, 'Possible candidate for lithium' for the morning clinical team to consider. This was solid, straightforward mental health care, and here he was, secure in his knowledge and recommendations.

But it was now nearly ten o'clock, and the late June evening was only just holding on to its vestiges of daylight.

He was tired but satisfied, looking forward to a meal in his new home in Medenby, a much more comforting place to be than the sombre Victorian flat in the hospital.

He breathed a mixture of contentment and satisfaction as he drove out past the entrance pillars of Middleshire Hospital. It had been a difficult day, but he had coped well. Soon he reached Checkpoint D at the southern entrance, where he was quickly waved through. A few minutes later he was driving up the long drive that ended as a cul-de-sac. Yes, he and Pauline had chosen well for their first proper home. Few people came beyond the last junction in the drive, which meant they had the opportunity to get to know their neighbours and Patrick was safe to play out of doors.

He drew up outside his new house, number 94, and parked. Had he noticed some figures in the gathering dusk? Odd, nobody was normally around at this time. Must be some meeting nearby. He switched off the ignition, put up the handbrake, picked up his briefcase and opened the car door. The figures drew closer. What was going on? There seemed to be at least four of them, coming towards him, menacing in the half light.

'Hey, mate, come here,' someone shouted.

Stephen turned towards the sound.

'Crazy, are we, you bastard? Who the bloody hell do you think you are? God?'

He felt he had to respond. He approached a young man in a donkey jacket. He must calm these people down. 'Let me explain.'

But he never did explain. The man behind him made sure of that. As his baseball bat completed its arc and struck Stephen's skull, there was a blinding flash across his brain. He slumped to the ground. He felt his head being kicked over and over before consciousness was lost completely.

TWENTY-EIGHT

DAY EIGHTY-ONE, NO NEW CASES

Reflection, you may come tomorrow,
sit by the fireside with Sorrow

Percy Bysshe Shelley, 1822

Barbara was devastated by Stephen's assault. She also felt ashamed about her previous provocative behaviour in his car; why had she been so brazen? Was she over-sexed, or even vampish? Could her behaviour have had anything to do with what had happened to Stephen? No, no matter how she puzzled about it, there was no possible connection. On reflection she did not regret that circumstances had led to the failure of the tryst with Stephen. She had persuaded herself that once her virginity had been lost there was no further need for any sexual connection. But would it? Could the taking of an aphrodisiac once lead to addiction over time? It was a question she was glad she was not going to have to answer.

She tentatively entered the ward at visiting time. Good, there was nobody by his bed: no relatives, no hospital colleagues. But she hardly recognised him. His head was tightly bandaged, his face was swollen and there was a large purple bruise surrounded by stitches in his left cheek.

But he was awake, and he recognised her and smiled. 'Sorry we missed our rendezvous.'

'Don't mention it. I feel awful thinking about it now. It just seems in a different world, but I do want to apologise.'

'Whatever you do, my dear Barbara, do not apologise. I remember it fondly; what happened and what didn't happen are both equally important. Passionate sex can be foolish ecstasy, better contemplated than performed. But I am getting pompous. And you are right about secrecy. Nobody should know apart from us.'

Barbara was pleased; the difficult part of the meeting was over. She leant down and kissed him on his bandaged head. 'Now, nobody can complain about that, can they? But what is going to happen to you? How long are you going to be in hospital? Can you continue your work on Poleaxe?'

'Help. I can't deal with all these questions. They'll give me a headache, and as you can imagine, that's the last thing I need just at this moment. What I do know is that I have had a bleed into the back of my head after I was attacked, and that I am going to need plastic surgery and bone reconstruction on my cheek. My concentration is still not back to normal either.'

Barbara had to interrupt. 'But you are going to be able to work again?'

'Yes, but not for many months. They are sending me to a special rehabilitation unit sixty miles away. So I'll be out of commission, but not completely. I can still think, though a bit sluggishly at times, and I'll keep in touch with Giles, so I'll know what's going on. I think I may have told you, I'm pretty determined, and I want see this Poleaxe problem seen through to the end.' He smiled at Barbara, checking she was listening.

'Absolutely. I'm a stubborn so-and-so as well, and I'm not letting go. I'm not nearly as clever as you doctors, but I'm sure I can help.'

'Your contribution has been more than you will ever know – I suppose I don't completely mean that – but because you see everything from a fresh angle you see things that we don't. You remind me at times of Leonardo da Vinci – don't let that go to your head – who, because he had no other training apart from his inner talent and observational skills, achieved so much more than the scientists of his time.'

Barbara was flattered. It was not often she was praised for her intellect, but she suspected the pedestal on which she was being placed was unduly high. Perhaps his damaged brain, and his relationship with her, had passed a cloud over his judgement.

'I can't live up to that, but I will continue to try, and I am so pleased you have let me into your world.'

Barbara could see Stephen was getting tired, and their conversation had run its course.

But Stephen had something else to say. 'Before you leave, could you just let me hold your hand for a few seconds?'

Barbara readily complied. He held it and then slowly turned her wrist and stroked the delicate palm with his other hand.

'Thank you, Barbara. It may be some time before I see you again and I needed something to remember.'

As Barbara walked out she could see that Stephen would soon have another visitor. It was James Porton, head down and concentrating. He walked straight past her without looking up.

Thank goodness for that, thought Barbara, as she walked towards the hospital bus stop. *He wouldn't want to see me after all this trouble, even though I doubt he would recognise me now.*

The bus soon arrived, noisy and familiar, and as usual she moved to sit on the back seat so she could see everybody. Looking at passengers from the back seat was a good anthropological exercise. There they were, in predictable form. There were the housewives, chatting inconsequentially, mainly about prices of food items; schoolgirls giggling about the boys just in front of them, who in their turn tried to look at them surreptitiously from behind their seats, failing universally to avoid being seen, and only leading to shrieks of high-pitched delight. On the left she heard older men telling stories about the past in a continuous drone. Everything was almost back to normal. It was good to see that they were no longer so alarmed about Poleaxe and able to travel freely.

But what was going to happen with the Poleaxe investigation now? Stephen was going to be off the scene and only Giles was aware of all the ramifications of the syndrome. It was receding and new cases were now very rare, but it still remained a mystery. What was she able to do now, especially as she would be off to live in college soon? The bus trundled its way back to Medenby town centre, past the Manse where she would get off. But for what? Back to the restrictions of life with Pamela Dukinfield? Definitely not. She would keep her mind fixed on Poleaxe and anthropology, and she must devour any clues that crossed her path. A proper scientist she may not be, but she was determined to be more than just a camp follower.

TWENTY-NINE

DAY EIGHTY-ONE, NO NEW CASES

*The words of psychiatry are often unjust stewards, sorry
guardians of meaning, workers of deception*

Aubrey Lewis, psychiatrist, 1934

He had to do it. He didn't want to, but it needed to be
done. He had to visit Stephen in hospital. The crushing
weight of responsibility bore down like a deep persistent
headache. Of course he had nothing to do with the attack
on Stephen, but there was a niggling admonition ringing
inside his head that somehow, had he behaved differently,
all this could have been avoided. So he had muscled up his
courage and made the decision.

'I shouldn't have shut my mind to mental illness.' he
muttered to himself as he drove to the hospital. 'It's not
as though it's a stranger.' The episode had reawakened the
memory of that awful occasion when he was sixteen. He
should never have allowed himself to be persuaded by his
father.

'It's the right decision, James. Whatever you think of the armed services if you are in the Cadet Force at school, you will become an officer when you are called up to do your national service.'

So he had been persuaded, and one of the requirements was to go on a summer camp. And there he'd been, in glorious weather at the end of July when he should have been lazing by the beach or swimming in the sea off the Welsh coast. Instead he'd been at a military camp in an airfield in the middle of that flat and uninspiring county, Lincolnshire. He had got out of the bus. What a miserable scene it had been. It was as though God had given his apprentice the first go at creating a country. A totally flat landscape, in monochrome green, with the odd hedge to break up the line. In the middle, a two-dimensional building with scores of identical windows separated by grey columns. The only things missing were toy soldiers strutting woodenly about, but they were imitated well by khaki identikit equivalents. How ghastly and impersonal, and what a place to spend the next two weeks?

The cadets had been billeted in wooden huts in the corner of the airfield. They'd been left alone in the evenings and spent long hours lying on their bunks at night, talking. Their conversations had been primitive, revolving mainly about stories about dunking larger and larger volumes of spunk into the vaginas of the girls of their sister school. Of course, James and everybody else had known these were almost all fantasies – where were all those teenage pregnancies? – but when the occasional account carrying even a smidgeon of truthfulness had been identified, it was explored and dissected at length. James had taken no part in these nightly verbal rambles; he'd felt embarrassed and uncomfortable, and the others despised him for his failure to join in. So he was gradually cold-shouldered and ignored.

Six days into the camp, he'd been woken in the middle of the night by four of the other boys.

'Up you get, Porton, we have a pleasant surprise for you,' a disembodied voice had sneered.

James had only been in state of semi-understanding, but when two others stripped him roughly, he'd been forced to wake. A fourth had rubbed something into his testicles. His arms had been grabbed and he was frog-marched out of the hut.

He'd been terrified. 'Where are you taking me, and what is all this for?' he'd stammered pathetically.

'As you are a stain on humanity, Porton, we have decided to show humanity where you are stained. You are now blackballed.'

He'd been bundled into a tennis court close to the huts. Someone had managed to get hold of a key. James had heard the lock click and the four boys had slunk away. He'd walked round to find another exit. There was none, so he'd crouched in a corner of the court, utterly bereft and alone. He'd cursed the day he was born human; any other animal would be better treated. He could find no explanation for this primitive exercise in humiliation. Yes, he was not very tall, was socially inept, was always on the edge of things, but how could any of these be a reason for such cave-mannish and brutal behaviour?

Fortunately it had been a warm night – the boys had thought of everything – but there had been no possibility of sleeping. Several times he'd had to move to different parts of the court when ants started crawling round his toes. He could not remember if any were flesh-eating, but his mind was going to interpret the worst of every scenario, and even the slow-moving woodlice that took to exploring his groin were viewed as rapacious monsters.

So sleep had stayed far away, and when, at the early arrival of daylight, one of the boys, perhaps regretting his earlier actions, had come to let him out, he could only nod his thanks, climb back into his pyjamas and bury himself so deeply in his bunk that nobody would guess he was there.

But still the trouble had still not been over. He had not talked about this experience to anybody when he returned home – who on earth could? As the days had crept on towards the return to school in September, he'd felt mounting dread. And when he'd gone in on the first day, during a lesson in the same class as his torturers, he'd had an acute attack of panic that could not be suppressed. He could not get his breath, his heart had been beating so hard it felt it would escape from his chest, he had been shaking all over, and the tingling in his hands and feet had led to complete cramp in his muscles. He'd collapsed in his chair and had to be escorted to the sick room.

Of course it had all been hushed up as a problem following 'something he had eaten' and he'd returned to school the next day. But it took over a year to restore a modicum of self-confidence and a determination not to let people take advantage of him in the same way again. And during this time, he'd had many dark thoughts, including those of suicide, that he'd kept away from everybody; he had been so ashamed of himself for reasons he could not understand.

As he went into the ward, this memory was twisting in his brain. It was aggravated further by seeing Stephen, vulnerable and damaged, in his hospital bed. *This is how I was, all those years ago. Lost, scared, unsettled, and this time responsibility is partly mine.*

He found it difficult to talk. 'Felt I had to come and see you. Never expected anything like this. Very sorry about everything.' The words were being dragged from him.

Stephen was disinclined to help. 'It's happened now, and I'm out of the danger tunnel.'

James continued to struggle. 'I never intended any harm. It was just… like a deflection from the inquiry… making people confused… wouldn't make sense to everybody.'

'So you thought people would think Poleaxe was just mass hysteria?'

'No, I never thought that. But I thought you were out of your depth in saying that anxiety might be a cause.' James thought this comment was hypercritical and needed to qualify. 'I mean, you might not have been able to grasp the implications.'

It was clear Stephen was getting exasperated, or tired, or both. 'Dr Porton, as you can see, I am not well because of my injuries and my concentration is faulty. I am not exactly sure what you want and if we are to get anywhere, I need you to be clearer in your intentions. Can I simply ask, why are you here?'

James was jolted into attention. He realised he had to come clean. 'I admit I was rude when I met you in my office. I wrongly assumed you did not know what you were talking about. I also have to admit that in the past I have had my own mental health problems, but I suppress them and try to avoid the subject. So this probably came into my head when I saw you. I suppose you must have come across this before.'

'Yes.' Stephen smiled ruefully. He was more sympathetic now. 'Those who attack psychiatry often have the most need for its ministrations. It is a difficult subject, but its fundamentals are very clear.'

Stephen wanted to get an important message over to him. He sat up and looked hard at James. 'A science based primarily on self-report, interview and observation can never escape allegations that it is bogus. This is why scientologists and other critics have so much ammunition to use against psychiatry. Mental distress is very real, and whether we regard it as an illness, a reaction to events or just a bigger down among the ups of life, does not really matter. We just have to acknowledge it is there. Whatever the level of evidence, nobody can deny mental illness exists.'

James had to agree. His experiences in darkest Lincolnshire were certainly real.

'The reason we try to hide mental illness is all to do with shame. For some reason, mental illness is something for which we continue to blame ourselves. This is another reason why people like the scientologists do so well. They help to export shame. They are able to project it to other people, like psychiatrists and others who work in mental health services. If you can persuade people that their problems are wrongly diagnosed by professionals who only want phoney reasons to draw their salaries, you have open season for gullibility.'

Stephen was now staring hard at James. He wanted to make sure he was getting his points home.

'It is pernicious. This is why our Minister of Health, Kenneth Robinson, is trying to ban the scientologists. Note that we don't make people who develop lung cancer after smoking feel ashamed for being ill, even though we have warned them about the risks. We sympathise. But with mental illness we shame and blame. We prefer not to admit we have been unwell and then blame others if we have no other choice.'

James was forced to agree. He was now able to open up a little more and was beginning to understand. But he still had doubts.

'There's another source of trouble. In medicine, when we make diagnoses or predictions about disease, we expect to be able to back up what we say by independent tests or biological evidence that nobody can dispute. It's not like that with mental illness.'

'I fully understand that difficulty. But because we describe someone as being depressed, anxious, paranoid, psychotic, deluded or any of the many other words we bandy about in our profession, it does not mean that there is no substance underlying them. You have mentioned that you have had your own mental health problems. I do not want to pry, but I am sure you have used these loaded words to describe to yourself your own problems in the past. By using these words, you are giving some sort of approximation to the truth; the fact that you use them does not make them any the less real. Some people are literally scared to death because of the intensity of their anxiety. We have even come across this in cases of Poleaxe. But you will never see "fear" or "anxiety" on their death certificates. But if we had a blood test or investigation that unequivocally measured "severe anxiety", then this could be put on the certificate. It would then be a medical condition.'

James was now deeply involved in a subject that had bothered him ever since his teenage experiences. 'Is there any reason why we cannot have a blood test now? We are making major advances in technology.'

'I think it highly unlikely. Although words like "depression" and "anxiety" are highly subjective – one person may minimise while the other may exaggerate – they are still the best measure of emotion. So if you had a blood test that indicated you were not depressed but you still complained of all the symptoms of depression, we would have to conclude the test was wrong.'

'This is where I have had difficulty with Poleaxe. You have said anxiety is a major factor, but you cannot measure it. I was in the same position with Poleaxe when all I had to go on was a disease that spread rapidly. Until we found a viral cause, the infection idea was only a hypothesis. Your theory will forever remain a hypothesis until you have a test.'

'Dr Porton. I am tired now and think we have talked long enough. What you really need to ask yourself is whether the symptoms of mental illness you had all those years ago were just a hypothesis, as you put it, or a genuine manifestation of distress. Once you have decided, you have the answer.'

Stephen lay back on his two raised pillows and closed his eyes. It was a clear indication the conversation was over. James stayed a little longer. He had underestimated Stephen. He was intelligent and thought a lot about his subject, and it was something that was part of medicine. He had to make up for his past errors.

'Thank you for this discussion, Dr Bollider.' He still could not call him 'Stephen'. 'You have convinced me that mental symptoms must be part of Poleaxe. I hope I have your support in taking this forward.'

Stephen did not open his eyes. 'Of course, we need as many disciples as possible.'

THIRTY

DAY EIGHTY-FOUR, NO NEW CASES

Dreams are true while they last and do we not live in dreams.

Alfred, Lord Tennyson, 1869

Barbara was growing in strength and confidence, and felt that she must continue the work that had been started with Stephen. She still yearned to see him but realised there would be no possibility of meeting him again. But there were other things on her mind too. She had to catch up on her anthropology studies, as nearly two months had been lost from her course. She was still confined to hospital, but this was only because the hospital feared others might still be infected and had nothing to do with her degree of recovery, which was now almost complete. They would make some allowances for Poleaxe in her department at Nottingham University, but if she fell too far behind, she might never catch up.

There was an urgent task needing to be done before the end of the month. She had to complete her special project on the life and times of the Orang Asli, the oldest tribe in Malaysia. As she had mentioned to Mrs Unwin, it had always fascinated her that tribes in the middle of one of the busiest trade routes in the world had somehow managed to keep their identity. It hadn't happened in the British Isles: no Viking warriors, Neolithic farmers or early Celts had survived for anthropologists like her to study. She wanted to find out how, and why, these tribes had survived in Malaysia.

So Dad had brought her papers from home, giving her great encouragement, and she was nicely set up in the dayroom with no interruption. Nurse Grant, who had quietly mentioned that her first name was Jane, so Barbara knew she had made a friend, made sure she would not be disturbed.

What made the Orang Asli so determined to hold on? Barbara asked herself. Her papers gave her some clues. One part of the tribe, the Senoi, fascinated her. They lived high up in the jungle forests and were seldom disturbed by the comings and goings of the people below. So why did they stay where they were? Didn't they want to explore the world below? As Barbara read, she was beginning to find out why. They used dreams to control their lives. Yes, dreams. They didn't ignore dreams or analyse their hidden significance like psychoanalysts; they made them work for the tribe's benefit. They shared them with everybody and had strategies for putting them into practice. Most importantly, they used them to predict what was going to happen.

Barbara tingled with enthusiasm as she read on. She imagined the tribe sitting cross-legged at breakfast. The elder spoke. 'Now for the jobs of the day. Let's get down to dream-sharing. Who would like to start? Don't be shy. Tell me about all of them. Which one of you has a really important dream to put us in the picture?'

So Barbara could imagine them talking if they had been faced with Poleaxe. 'We are confronted by a hidden danger. Has anyone had a dream that has faced danger? Has anyone collapsed or died? Did the dream show a way forward? What can we all learn from it?'

This seemed an ideal way of dealing with uncertainty, rather better than Medenby was doing at the moment. And it didn't matter if the Senoi forest people were wrong in their dream work. Because they all concurred, because they shared all their beliefs and fantasies, they were equipped to deal with adversity. Whether they were fatalists or optimists did not matter; their response was a common one. They worked together.

As a consequence, they were at peace and harmony with themselves, and it was written clearly, in all the documents she could find, that they never experienced mental illness. They were the first-time travellers, knowing what would happen in advance because they had experienced it already and so were immune from surprise. So Barbara had to get this down, cogently and clearly, in her essay.

'The Senoi tribe in the Cameron Highlands of Malaysia are a paradox,' she started. Yes, that was a good first sentence. 'They are among the most primitive in their lifestyle but among the most advanced in the way they look at the future. By using the collective experience of their dreams, they plan each day and all their expectations are met.'

She was aware of someone behind her. It was Jane Grant.

'Looks as though you're getting on a treat with that,' she said.

'Yes, I am, Jane. And, as you are here, I have a question. Do you think that we can work out the future by looking at our dreams?'

Jane laughed. 'Well, mine wouldn't add anything to the sum of human knowledge. They're so boring everyone would go to sleep if I repeated them.'

This did not satisfy Barbara. She persisted. 'But this tribe I'm writing about in my project, they share all their dreams, and, taken together, they make up a story that helps them to foretell the future. It's not the individual dreams that matter; it's their combination that shows the way forward. It sounds crazy, but it seems they've been doing this for thousands of years.'

'Well, the best of luck to them. But, as for me, I'm happy for the future to give me a few surprises. Anyway, it's time for lunch now. Not many surprises there.'

She whisked away in her brisk and efficient manner. Barbara gathered up her notes, still thinking hard, wanting someone to take this subject more seriously.

After lunch all the patients in Block G were required to have an afternoon nap. 'Fourteen winks,' Jane told Barbara. Matron Arbuthnot reminded her staff, 'Not as much as forty, but just right to restore the body.' She was a great believer in sleep, although she did not have enough time to embrace it herself. So Barbara and the others took to their beds, the curtains were drawn, the lights dimmed, and silence descended.

She was climbing through the jungle, barefoot. The sun was high above, but the trees excluded most of the light. Dry leaves littered the ground and crackled as they were crushed underfoot. It was very hot. She noticed that both Danny and Stephen were with her. Good, that made her feel better. This was a most unusual place. As they climbed higher, it got even hotter and the breeze they were expecting never came. She could hear her mother calling in the distance. She wanted her to come back down, but it was more exciting going on.

Suddenly the ground gave way beneath them and all three of them were tossed down, down and further down, slowly, floating through the branches, into a shallow pool. Her mother's voice was very faint now. The pool was cool, but as she lay it became warmer, uncomfortably warmer. She noticed Danny and Stephen were lying in the pool too, but strangely detached from each other.

As the water became warmer still she felt her clothes sticking, close, cloying and uncomfortable. She could not tolerate them irritating her body. She pulled off her bra, dress and knickers; they were alien garments, no longer needed. Danny and Stephen, one on each side of her, seemed to be doing the same. She was pleased. They rolled out of the pool and lay on a shallow bank, looking at each other's naked bodies. She realised she had never examined the naked body of a man before. The two men seemed interested in her body too.

Above the waist they were very different but below they were very much the same, except around the crotch, where their hair distribution differed around a prominent object. Had this any significance for her anthropological studies? Could tribes be classified by their genitalia? She must make a note of this important question when she returned home. But something else was happening. Both men were turning towards her. Which one would she kiss first? Desire and uncertainty mingled together, and everything was moist below.

Barbara awoke, hot and twitching all over, but strangely serene inside. Yes, she had lost her anxiety. The Senoi were right. Their dreams freed them from mental illness. This dream work certainly had something going for it. She hoped she would have many more dreams, just like this. But how would the Senoi tribe have liked her to proceed? They would have wanted her to share this experience with all the others. She understood, but would fuller discussion of this dream help to solve the Poleaxe problem? Her contemplation was short. She thought not. Sharing dreams was admirable, but not always wise. This particular dream she would keep close to herself, but it may have ramifications.

CHAPTER THIRTY-ONE

DAY NINETY

Rejection is a blade to the heart. It's the worst kind of pain

Toni Sorenson, 2011

The Poleaxe Task Group meetings were nearing their end. There had been no new cases for many days. The purpose of the meetings had been served. The numbers had also diminished, and only William Fothergill, Charles Merridew, Barclay and Patterson, together with James, were present at today's meeting. James was not looking forward to the likely revelations following the attack on Stephen Bollider, but he was determined to see it through. He had to keep his nerve.

He arrived early, but William Fothergill was already there. He smiled at James, a hard, cold smile that showed something was afoot. But James was not prepared for what followed.

'James, I thought I should tell you that I am going to chair this particular meeting. I have also asked Giles

Camberwell to come. I know he has been helping you with Poleaxe, but in recent weeks I have asked to see him regularly too.'

'But I had no idea of this. Why didn't you let me know?'

'I will explain later, James. I think you will find it is for the best.'

For the best, James said to himself. This odious man had made a decision, on his own, without any consultation, and then embraced it as 'for the best', implying that all would agree with his personal, unilateral choice. This was the acme of arrogance. But what could he do? He had to keep focused and resolved.

The others straggled in, Giles included. James tried to catch his eye but did not succeed.

William took control. 'Thank you for coming. Important developments have taken place in the last few weeks and I feel it best for me to chair this meeting. I have invited Dr Giles Camberwell to this meeting as he has new information we all ought to know. This concerns a new way we have of dealing with people who have Poleaxe. Giles, could you update us?'

'Thank you, Dr Fothergill. Until now we have not had any treatment for the Poleaxe Syndrome. We have found out that it fluctuates but have not been able to understand why. My conversations with Dr Stephen Bollider, whom you know has recently been assaulted but I am glad to say is now recovering, suggested that if we reduced patients' level of anxiety it could be beneficial. So I tested this hypothesis by giving intravenous Valium to one of the patients who had remained paralysed since admission. This was successful in that the patient was able to move her arms and legs again, if only temporarily. We therefore think that reduction of anxiety is an important part of management.'

'But you must know that Valium and other benzodiazepines have a direct effect on muscles as well as reducing anxiety,' Charles Merridew interjected.

'Yes, but we have other evidence that high anxiety levels aggravate this condition.'

'Are you really saying that this medical disorder is one of anxiety?' asked Dr Barclay. 'That is nonsense. It paralyses people. It kills them. Are you saying they are just scared to death?'

'No,' replied Giles patiently. 'We have established that Poleaxe is caused by some sort of infectious agent, probably a virus, but whether or not it leads to the disease seems to depend on the mental state of the people affected.'

'I think that conclusion is a reasonable one.' The smooth Fothergill voice could iron out every argumentative wrinkle. 'Your research has been most impressive, Giles. We must write a paper about this as soon as we can.'

Typical Fothergill, thought James. *He has done nothing to investigate the syndrome and yet will claim all the credit for the publications.* He wanted to interrupt, but William was in full control.

'But there is another matter that I would like to bring up at this point. We are all aware that Dr Porton has been under considerable strain in the last few days because of the recent events already alluded to. He has also expressed reservations about the cause of Poleaxe that we fully understand. The public health element of Poleaxe has now been settled, due in no small measure to the valiant efforts of Dr Porton and his team. I am sure all members of the group would like to acknowledge this contribution.'

He paused briefly and beamed at James with total insincerity. 'But in the light of recent developments, we think it best that he no longer remains a member of this group.'

James was expecting something, but not this. 'But I am fully on board with this inquiry. And I have just seen Dr Stephen Bollider, who is very happy for me to be involved.'

'What Dr Bollider feels is completely irrelevant. He has no connection with the inquiry,' was William's acid reply.

James had to try another tack. 'But you have made this decision without approval from others. This is not an agreed arrangement. What do others feel?'

'You forget, James. We are all members of the Hospital Management Committee and have discussed this already.'

James now realised this was a stitch-up. He should have just walked out, but he had to make a speech first, an unnecessary one and one that would not help his cause. He was boiling with anger and it had to be released.

'I should have expected this. To you, we in public health are just the foot-soldiers of the medical army. We scour about in the distant undergrowth, trying to prevent and identify disease while you generals in the hospital sit back and wait for the accolades as you defeat illness by your standard medicines. So you can dismiss us in an afterthought, as we lose our importance once the diseases roll in. But you are wrong, utterly wrong, as we are the custodians of health. We prevent more deaths in a week than you do in a year with your fancy treatments. So you may dismiss me today, but you will require us again tomorrow, but next time you will have to come begging.'

He stood and swivelled on his heel, like all good foot-soldiers should, and walked out.

'Thank you so much for your contribution, James.' The mellifluous tones of William Fothergill accompanied him out of the door.

THIRTY-TWO

DAY ONE HUNDRED

From quiet homes and first beginning
Out to the undiscovered ends
There's nothing worth the wear of winning
But laughter and the love of friends

Hilaire Belloc, 1923

It was time for Barbara to leave hospital for good. The summer had been pretty miserable but on this late July day the balmy morning air hinted at a very warm day to come. Barbara tasted the light breeze and lolled in the cadence of the birdsong in the nearby elms as she walked outside Block G. Yes, she would leave the building with many memories, some that she could bask in, others that were the stuff of nightmares. It was how she imagined a boarding school could be, although she had never been in one. Frightening and threatening at first, but then getting better steadily as she cultivated new friendships, but always with a hint of menace that distress could return at any time. But it was good that all these recollections could be stashed away in her mind as those of a temporary residence. They would all be replaced.

But would home be different now? It seemed an age since she had been there, and now she was completely changed. Would her little bedroom at the top of the house be recognisable? Would Mum try to drag her back to the old routine of church duties clothed in cloying commitment? Would she be allowed to exercise her new role as a young woman without restraint? It was impossible to tell, but she was quite determined to assert her new independence, and, if ructions came, she would not be diverted.

Robert and Pamela Dukinfield had arrived early. They too were keen to have their daughter home as soon as possible. The reliable Morris Traveller was parked outside, its wood polished and bodywork gleaming in the sun. Barbara made her goodbyes to the staff. Most of them had been with her from the start, had seen her change from an inert corpse-like figure to a constant friendly presence on the ward. She shook hands with the nursing assistants and ward orderlies, ordinary Medenby folk with no pretensions but with hearts of innate goodness. 'Sorry you're going, duck, you're like one of us now,' said one of them. Jane Grant was unfortunately off duty, but Matron Arbuthnot was also there to say goodbye to Barbara.

Despite her intimidating presence, Barbara had grown to like her over the months she had been in the ward. She was organised and efficient, but also caring. Jane had told Barbara that Miriam was a Nightingale, not a title given for her singing, but only attached to the nurses trained at St Thomas's Hospital in London for an extra year of training. This was a true badge of distinction that could not be denied.

'Glad you're now well, Dukerfield. But don't overexert yourself. Moderation without stagnation are the watchwords.'

Barbara felt privileged to be seen off by Miriam Arbuthnot, even if she could never remember her name, but decided not to give her a hug, for fear of being crushed by those muscular arms. Instead she curtsied – only slightly, but still a curtsy – to show her respect.

In only a short time, she was home.

Pamela was gushing with attention, fussing over her daughter. 'You can't believe how excited we are to have you back home again, darling. They're all waiting too at the church garden this afternoon. They insisted on having a sing-song welcome home party for you, so we've got a group of singers who are going to make us all join in those marvellous songs from *Oklahoma!*.' Pamela could not stop herself from expressing herself in Oklahomian – 'Oh, What a Beautiful Mornin''. Fortunately she stopped at this point. She was wobbling off tune and could never hit the high notes of 'beautiful feeling' that followed.

Barbara was mortified. She was expecting a quiet day at home getting adjusted. Instead she would be whisked away to an event where she would have to be smiling insincerely, making sure she talked to all the people her parents thought she should be talking to, joining in revelry she did not share and having no time to herself. But her new maturity forced her to think a little longer. Mum was well-meaning but limited; she had little understanding of her daughter so wrongly thought she would like such a homecoming, and would be very upset if Barbara recoiled and reacted badly. So she would grit her teeth, play the game and see it through.

In reacting to this news, Barbara also realised something else had changed. In the past, when news like this had been sprung on her, she would have panicked and thought immediately about all that could go wrong and what she had to do to avoid catastrophe.

The questions would always be the same. Who would be upset if she did not acknowledge them? What might she wear that would cause offence? Was there anything she was expected to say (in which case she would have to rehearse the speech in advance)? And that most difficult of decisions – when do you stay in the background or come into the front?

Now she understood that these questions were unnecessary, and actually futile. She would just be herself, and people would have to take her as the Barbara Dukinfield she was, not another Barbara that they would like her to be. And in coming to this conclusion she acknowledged something else. She was no longer anxious, no longer expecting tragedy or threat around every corner. Her grandmother had said to her, probably from her own experiences, 'If it's nervous you're born, it's nervous you'll die, and in the middle you'll need to be held.' But Barbara now disputed this; she no longer needed to be held, by anyone. So the idea that she had a permanently anxious disposition was probably wrong. Perhaps personalities could change. It would be excellent if this were indeed true.

Within an hour they were off to the welcoming party. The afternoon was turning out to be unbearably warm and humid, and Barbara regretted her choice of the bright red flared dress she had chosen to wear. There were already more than forty people at the garden next to the church, and a cheer rang out when the Dukinfield family arrived. Barbara smiled demurely and gave a casual wave.

Richard Spowin was the minister chosen to be master of ceremonies. Barbara liked him. He came from Northern Ireland and had a megaphone voice and boundless energy. He had erected the stage for the invited players virtually on his own and Barbara was not at all surprised. She often had to ask him to slow down. Already he was more active than everybody else.

'Richard, slow down. Rome wasn't built in a day, you know.'

'That's because I wasn't there,' was the response, as he lugged a large beam to fix to the back of the stage.

Before long he was ready to introduce the band. 'Welcome all to this celebration of the return of our daughter, Barbara, from the shadow of death to the light of the living,' he boomed like an Ian Paisley impression.

'But this is an occasion for celebration, not speeches, and we have an afternoon of songs, hymns and luscious cakes to look forward to. So let me first introduce our players, the Oklahoma OK Methodist People's Hymnody, which in case you hadn't noticed, spells OOMPH, and I can tell you all, folks, we are going to be full of oomph over the next few hours. Over to you, lads, bring it on!'

The four singers, with their guitars and an accordion, waved and strummed an introduction.

Barbara was pleased they would all be singing hymns also. She agreed with that sensible voice of Methodism,

Lord Soper, that it was a tragedy that the children of today were singing songs from the radio instead of the hymns that were sung by their forebears. And with Rodgers and Hammerstein belting out their great tunes from *Oklahama!*, it was bound to be fun. She was now determined to enjoy herself, even though her dress was now sticking to her. Others were commenting on her marvellous figure, but there was a limit to perfect contours when they exposed your full anatomy.

The afternoon became even hotter, and among the crowd thronged in the garden the sweat penetrated every garment inexorably and damp patches spread in all the likely, and some unlikely, places. Barbara was beginning to find the heat unbearable but as she only had a one-piece dress, she had no choice but to keep it on, opening the buttons at the front sufficiently to hide her cleavage. Officially, as with all such events in the Methodist church, there was no alcohol allowed, but someone had doctored the orange juice with homemade cider and many, without realising it, were getting a little tipsy.

Alan Arkwright, a tall and gangly lad with a tendency to facial acne, was one of Barbara's secret admirers, always trying to sit next to her at services and mooning around her without having the courage to say anything. But in the heat of the afternoon, and encouraged by the Rodgers and Hammerstein lyrics and her wet and inviting figure, he became less secret, found her on her own, lurched forward and kissed her, saying her lips were like cherries, and he wanted to taste more. Barbara liked him and did not want to offend. She told him that her sweating lips and running lipstick were now more like a smear of raspberry jam, but allowed him a few kisses without opening her mouth, and then laughingly pushed him away.

'You think I'm a girl that can't say no, Alan, but I can.'

And who was that over in the distance? Yes, it was Jane Grant. Barbara rushed over.

'You're the last person I expected.' She gave her the biggest of hugs.

'I saw the event on the pole outside and just had to come. I was born in Wales and just love a good sing-song, and it's even better to know it's for you. So you couldn't keep me away. And in any case, I wanted to see you to say how much you've helped us all on the ward in the last few months. You really made the place hum.'

Barbara protested. 'That can't be true.'

'Yes, it is. I don't think you realise what a talent you've got for cheering everybody up. It just comes with you, without any effort. I'm sure you'll make the most of it now.'

Wasn't it odd how people praised her for different reasons? Were they really all addressing the same Barbara Dukinfield?

As they both listened to the songs from *Oklahoma!*, Barbara thought of Medenby as an equivalent. Not all that much happened in Oklahoma apart from farming romances; not that much happened in Medenby either. It was a solid and staid town, or at least had been until the onset of Poleaxe. When the crowd, and Jane with Welsh gusto, decided to join in twisting the words of *Oklahoma* by singing 'Everything's up to date in Lincoln City', and, excruciatingly, forcing the word 'Medenby' into all the chorus lines. Nothing else seemed to matter in this crazy mix of buzz, good humour and joyous frenzy.

But now it was time for the hymns. Everyone knew them and so the voices almost drowned out the music-makers.

'And can it be that I should gain
An interest in the Saviour's blood.'

That fantastic hymn composed at the time of Charles Wesley's conversion always stirred Barbara to ardour. 'My chains fell off, my heart was free, I rose, went forth, and followed Thee'. It was just like Paul on the road to Damascus, complete acquiescence. How on earth could radio compete with that? She wished she could be converted so completely and convincingly, but she suspected it was unlikely to happen.

The crowd steamed, sang and savoured the heat of the afternoon with increasing abandon, and Barbara wondered why she had been so reluctant at first to embrace this homecoming. It was a great occasion, after all, and the pleasure people had shown towards her return was genuine, basic and unadorned.

And then they all sang, 'Love divine all loves excelling, joy of heaven to earth come down', with that line that Barbara had always tried to emulate, knowing she never would: 'pure and spotless let us be'. But never mind, she would try and keep the spots at bay.

It was getting late, but the enjoyment of the band and the singers ignored the tokens of time and bellowing beatitudes of praise continued to rise into the night, with the only semblance of order coming from the serried rows of high cumulus clouds shining pink in the last rays of the sun. But the party had to end eventually.

There was one more booming message from Richard Spowin. 'I know you're all roastin' now, but I would like us all to sing the last hymn for Barbara. She's back with us now and will be again. It's been a long time, but it's been worth it. So here's to the next time we see her. Let's sing "God be with you till we meet again".'

Barbara melted inside, and when they sang the verse:

'God be with you till we meet again,
When life's perils thick confound you
Put his arms unfailing round you
God be with you till we meet again,'

she was quite overcome with its sentiment, and the tears flowed, but without her feeling ashamed.

Jane was now ready to leave with the others. 'Don't forget they're opening the barriers tomorrow morning. I'll be at entrance A, hope you'll be there too.'

'Of course.' Barbara was getting intoxicated by the evening.

'Medenby new day will dawn before I go,' she sang in return.

But Reverend Richard Spowin had not quite finished. 'Look over there, girls,' he shouted, pointing towards the distant west, where the hills of the Derbyshire Peak District were just visible now the sun was almost set.

'I will raise my eyes up to the hills, from whence cometh my help. You've long lives ahead of you both. And I'll be watching you travel. Look up there now.' He too had been taken over by *Oklahoma!* and finished with a flourish about the blue moon in his rich baritone.

Jane and Barbara did indeed look up and saw the palest of blue-grey moons high in the sky above the dusk below. This was a marvellous ending.

Back at home, Pamela was completely enthused with her plans for Barbara.

'You must know, Barbara, from that marvellous homecoming that you are really treasured in the church. People are saying after all you've been through that you'd make a great local preacher. After all, you've nearly died and have been closer to God than most of us.'

Barbara was flattered but was not going to be diverted from her path forward now. 'Mum, that's something I might consider. But you may have forgotten, I will be going to college in six weeks' time. I simply cannot think about it now.'

'Of course, I understand, darling. But it is an honour. You would not need to be around every week and it could easily be fitted in. And it won't interfere with your studies.'

'Mum, I'm sorry, but it will. I need to tell you that I am now really interested in anthropology. I didn't think I would be, but the course has taught me an amazing amount and I really feel I could make a career in it.'

'But, darling, isn't anthropology just like all the other ologies. It's a way of getting a degree and useful letters after your name.'

'Absolutely not, or at least not for me. Anthropology has taught me about life in perspective and how we all behave in certain ways, many of them predictable, and that includes me and you. It going to be my focus for the immediate future, so please, Mum, back off.'

"Of course, darling, if you so wish.'

Pamela Dukinfield was seeing a new side to her beloved daughter. She would have to adapt.

THIRTY-THREE

DAY ONE HUNDRED AND ONE

Walls protect and walls limit.
It is in the nature of walls that they should fall

Jeanette Winterson, 1985

As far as Medenby was concerned, Poleaxe was over. There had been no new cases for nearly a month and life had returned to the familiar patterns of the past. Jobs to go to, some tedious but necessary, others promising and exciting, children finishing school and looking forward to their long summer holidays, young mothers showing off their babies in fancy, big-wheeled prams, and older people, no longer nervous to go out of doors, taking their morning constitutional walks with impunity – and talking to their neighbours close up.

Barbara saw examples of all of these as she walked up the Halton Road, past its fringing sycamores and horse chestnuts in the warm hazy sunshine to the A barrier. As she ran over the last few months in her mind, it still seemed extraordinary that she had been part of the whole Poleaxe process. If she hadn't been in the park just over four months ago she would have been like everybody else in Medenby: a worried spectator hoping to avoid the disease. Now she was involved in almost every episode of the drama, and the return of the town to the discourse of unimpeded traffic was a notable one. The four roadblocks in Medenby were now the only obstacles to the normal running of the town, and both central government and town council had agreed that they could now be removed. So the cranes were in position, the highways team with paving and road filling equipment were all ready, and the Lord Mayor, who lived only a short distance away, was ready to open the first of the four roads into the town.

A small knot of people was waiting and watching. A man with a banner saying 'Vote MIP' was haranguing the people waiting.

'What are you opening the road up for?' he shouted. 'We've got a much better life here without the rest of 'em muscling in. Vote for the Medenby Independence Party, the party that's going to put Medenby back on its feet, without all these foreigners from Nottingham and Lincoln.'

He was being received with some sympathy, but Jane, who was already at the barrier, and Barbara could not take him seriously. They could not wait for the road to be opened again. Medenby on its own would be stifling.

'All ready for the tin-opener?' Jane asked, laughing.

'Poleaxe on the way out, traffic on the way in.'

'It will certainly help our church congregation; many of them had given up coming.'

The Lord Mayor, like most of the town's officials, was not chosen for his oratory, and had to move off to open barrier D very soon afterwards, so once the barrier was moved and paving back in place, he made a short statement. 'I declare the Halton Road fully open.'

The small crowd waited for a more memorable statement, even a bland 'I now declare Medenby open for business'. But oratory was not what Medenby was noted for; it was not so much ignored but unrecognised. Plain speech would do perfectly well. He cut the ribbon and it fell away sadly to the ground, to be quickly trodden on.

'May God bless it and all who drive through her,' muttered Barbara to Jane, feeling the vacuum had to be filled.

The mayor and his entourage left, but Barbara and Jane stayed and chatted to the stallholders who had done good business outside the barrier for the last three months. They were keen to talk.

'Look over here, me ducks.' The young man wearing an apron showed them a row of oval buns on a table. 'You know what these are?'

'Some sort of roll?' suggested Jane.

'No,' said the man scornfully as he opened one of the buns to show a mixture of cream and some sort of jam inside. 'These are Medenby Muffins, or Double Ms. They may not look much, but they've made me hundreds of pounds, more than I ever make for my normal baking. People have a day out, come out to the barrier, have a good gossip, buy a load of muffins and tell all their friends about it when they get home. Then their friends come along and buy even more.'

He then introduced both of them to a friend who was selling bunches of long cheese sticks. Barbara looked at them closely. Each of them had a letter 'P' as a handle.

'And what on earth are these? Don't tell me. They must be Poleaxe sticks. Isn't that a bit tasteless?'

The other stall-holder was offended. 'Tasteless? You just try one. The tastiest cheese straws you'll ever find.'

Barbara and Jane each ate one.

'I have to agree,' Jane admitted as she demolished her own in two mouthfuls.

'Don't tell anyone,' said the stallholder, covering his mouth, 'but the cheese is not from Medenby. It's Stilton. I felt these Poleaxe straws had to knock you down to be real, so I made sure I had a powerful cheese.'

It was obvious these young entrepreneurs had been doing pretty well out of the crisis.

'So what are you going to do now? With the barrier gone, will you still have custom?'

'Naw. We'll pack up and go to our usual stands in Market Square. We won't do as well, but you never know. Now everyone can come into Medenby whenever they please, they might find it a novelty again. They might even get lost finding us. But when they do, they are bound to want a memento of Poleaxe, so we'll give it to them.'

But now there were customers arriving to buy, so the conversation was over.

Barbara made her farewells to Jane and walked back to the Manse. It was curious how a disaster for many could be an opportunity for others, and there seemed little doubt that there must be others in the town, unhappy for the barriers to go and sorry that ordinary life had to resume.

Enterprise flourishes in adversity, she thought, *and but for Poleaxe they would probably never have learnt the new skills they are likely to add to their repertoire.*

And of course they were not alone in that. She had developed so many new skills she could never have dreamt of a year ago. If anybody ever introduced her as 'a victim of Poleaxe', she would have to contradict them with, 'I am not a victim. I am a beneficiary of Poleaxe, and if you want to know why, I can tell you, but it may take some time.'

THIRTY-FOUR

DAY ONE HUNDRED AND TWENTY

Donner un sens plus pur aux mots de la tribu
(To give a purer sense to the language of the tribe)

Stéphane Mallarmé, 1865

The Famous Five first Poleaxe victims were having a reunion, but without Fred, whose loss they still mourned. There was an unusual bond created by medical adversity; this was even stronger when they had all suffered from the same disease. Now all the remaining four were well, with no ill effects from Poleaxe, and their meeting at the friendly café opposite the castle was a jolly affair.

Julia, Mary and Henry were all sitting at a table in the warm courtyard at the back of the café as Barbara arrived.

'Hi, Barbara, me duck,' said Mary. 'I'm glad you got me out today. It's good for the agoraphobia. But it's even better when Henry can come with me.'

'It helps me and all,' added Henry. 'Mary's a great companion.'

'So that's really exciting. Are you getting over your nervous problems together?'

Barbara liked the possibility of match-making and felt she would be good at it. Was this going to be one of her successes?

Henry and Mary interrupted each other in their haste to answer, but then Mary was given preference. 'I think you're right. When you suffer in tandem, you forget you suffer. So Henry and I do a lot together now. We even went to the cinema together the other evening.'

Each looked at the other with twitches of smiles. Barbara concluded they might have even held hands. But she was keen to talk further about Julia's experiences in Malaysia. The medical authorities had lost interest in her after dismissing the possibility that Japanese encephalitis might be the cause of Poleaxe. But Barbara was especially keen to know if she had met the Senoi tribe in the Cameron Highlands, and whether they were very different from others in the area.

'Yes, I visited the Cameron Highlands during my trip, but it was not a very enjoyable experience. I found it very odd. I was especially interested in going there as I am very keen on wild orchids, and there are over five hundred species of orchids there, more than any other part of Malaysia.'

Barbara did not want to lead her on too quickly to her own line of questioning. She had learnt from anthropology to let people speak as much as possible for themselves. But she had to give a nudge here and there.

'Were the people there very different from other parts of Malaysia?'

'Very different. The people there, a tribe that had been there for thousands of years, I think the name began with "S", had no interest in talking to us, unlike all the people from the other tribes.'

'Were they the Senoi tribe?'

'Yes, that's the name. I had one of their guides help me find some of the most unusual jungle orchids. He was very interesting but also very distant, because unlike the people from the other the tribes in the area he had absolutely no interest in me as a Westerner. He kept himself completely apart. I have done similar expeditions in Central Africa and at first our guides there were uncertain and careful about getting involved, but later we always became friends and could share a great deal, and sometimes even ate together.'

Julia was getting animated as she recalled these experiences. Barbara was impressed by her awareness and verve. She was a person to be reckoned with.

'So how was your Senoi guide different?'

Julia pursed her lips and wrinkled her nose. 'It's difficult to describe. He was completely secure in his own culture and experience, and had absolutely no wish to know about others. I actually found it a bit eerie. It was almost as though he was a different species, an alien in human clothing. He didn't seem to understand me, especially my interest in orchids, which I could understand as odd, but it was more than that. It was almost as though he despised me for not being the same as him. The normal deference these tribal people show towards foreigners, even if it is really designed to gain money, was completely missing. He treated me almost with disdain, as though I was unfortunate not to be like him.'

Barbara now had an entry for the questions that she really wanted to ask. 'In my work as an anthropologist – that sounds too pompous, as I'm only a student of the subject – I've found the Senoi tribe have a curious set of beliefs, which fundamentally come down to the idea that all their lives are predicted by their dreams. They share these and plan accordingly, and it seems that all their expectations are met. Does that make sense to you?'

'Well, Barbara, you have been doing your homework. It does make sense. My guide seemed to have an inner world that he had no intention of sharing with me.'

'And did you get the impression that he was really content in this inner world, and needed no other stimulation?'

'Absolutely. Although I found him irritating and nerve-wracking, he seemed completely serene. And of course that annoyed me even more. I was very pleased when he found the orchids I was looking for and left me to find my own way back to the more civilised places below.'

The four finished their tea and cakes in great harmony. Henry and Mary were going shopping together and Julia had an appointment with a travel agent – she was likely to be moving again soon – so Barbara was soon out on Castle Gate again. She was looking for a telephone box.

Yes, there was one. The red emblem in England's green and pleasant land. She knew Giles would be on call at the hospital and that they could call him on the tannoy. Yes, she pressed Button A in the call box and was through to the hospital. Giles was quickly contacted.

'Giles, you must let the Poleaxe team know something I have just discovered. I may be wrong, but I think the source of Poleaxe may be in the Cameron Highlands of Malaysia. That's where Julia Unwincroft was before she came back to Medenby via Singapore.'

'But what makes you think it was in that particular place?"

'It's too difficult to explain, but I know the experts are over in Malaysia and they must get the message to concentrate their efforts in the Cameron Highlands.'

'All right. I'll pass it on, but just in case you're wrong, I won't tell them where the idea came from.'

That was good enough for Barbara. She may well be wrong, but the Cameron Highlands were more than worthy of investigation.

THIRTY-FIVE

DAY ONE HUNDRED AND TWENTY-TWO

Thus repulsed, our final hope is flat despair

John Milton, 1667

James was making the pavlova when the call came. Although Elaine was the main cook in the Porton household, hardly surprising in view of her skills at every level, James was the pavlova expert. He had perfected this recipe over many years, but still kept it simple. The most important part was the cooking time at the right temperature, so much so that there was a special pavlova oven in the corner of the kitchen. He gradually whisked the caster sugar into the frothy egg whites, surely and methodically. Near the end, as the mixture stiffened into a true meringue he ensured that their sugary peaks rose like the domes of Russian orthodox churches around the central base. Once complete it could go into the pavlova oven at 140 degrees for exactly fifty minutes before the oven was switched off and the meringue allowed to dry gradually before being removed at least nine hours later.

The telephone rang at the last stage of preparation. Elaine answered. 'It's Harry, he wants to come over and have a talk with you.'

'That's very odd, why couldn't it wait until tomorrow?'

'He didn't say. But I said he could come straight over, as I suppose the pavlova will be in the oven by then.'

Elaine was perfectly capable of looking after the pavlova herself, but this was one task that James had to perform entirely alone.

The doorbell rang, one sound, ten seconds. Harry Berry, the Deputy Medical Officer of Health for Medenby, was let in by Elaine. James, sitting in the armchair opposite the door after settling the pavlova in its safe cooking station, noticed he was nervous. But of course, he hadn't visited him at home before and was bound to find it intimidating. Harry was very young and had been thrown by the gravity of Poleaxe, but he was beginning to understand.

'Could I have a word with you in private?' Harry stammered.

'Of course, but you must know I will share whatever you say with Elaine later.'

'I know, but I would feel more comfortable with you on your own.'

James rose and beckoned Harry to the small box room at the back of the house. It had been added on shortly after they had moved. James insisted that he had to have a study for his sensitive papers and so, even this addition was probably unnecessary it satisfied his whim for separate authority.

'So what's all the fuss about then?'

'It's about recent events.'

'I guessed it wouldn't be about more distant ones, come on, explain.'

'There have been a series of complaints made about your interview with David Frost. I cannot go into these in full detail, but essentially they claim you belittled psychiatrists, slandered Dr Bollider, and indirectly provoked the violent attack that lead to his admission to hospital.'

James was both flabbergasted and alarmed. Of course some people would be bound to indulge in primitive thinking when looking for people to blame, but this was going far too far.

'I have already made my peace with Dr Bollider about this issue, and said I was sorry, so why can't this be the end of the matter?'

'It could have been, but there were so many that in the end the county council and Medenby Hospital decided they had to take action.'

James exploded with anger. 'But that is none of their business. The hospital and the county council do not know anything about our department. We are independent.'

'But ultimately your salary is paid by the county council – you will remember this is the consequence of the rather antiquated system that has been around for years. It existed before the NHS was set up.'

Elaine came in with coffee and biscuits. Harry nodded and smiled in appreciation; James ignored her in his agitation.

'Never mind. But what have you come here to tell me about? Complaints are complaints. We get them all the time.'

'That's why I've come to see you. This time it's different.'

'Will you ever get to the point, Harry?'

Harry gulped. 'They have decided to have an inquiry, and in the meantime they have suspended you.'

James could not quite take this in. He first considered this quite literally. Where would he be suspended from, and who by? Would it be from the ceiling, would the hoi polloi be throwing stones at him as though in the stocks, or would he just spin around in isolation? And then it hit him – deep in the solar plexus of his being.

'They… they cannot do that. They do not have the power. And in any case, I can appeal. It is utterly disgraceful that they can treat me like this.'

'I'm sorry, James. They do have the power, and there is nothing you can do about it at this stage. They have decided to keep the subject under wraps, so no others will know about it, and of course they will ask you to testify.'

'So what am I meant to do? Sit around waiting for the bells to toll? Write my memoirs? Go away on a holiday for the first time in two years?'

'I really can't advise you on this, James. But I will be needing your advice as I will be running the department for the time being, and I will be in a sorry state without your help.'

'Of course. I need a break, but it would be wrong to go away for any length of time. But please, Harry, try and break it gently to the staff. Can you tell them I am just working from home for the time being?'

Harry became more animated.

'That's more or less what I've planned. They of course know that something is going on, but I've not mentioned the word "suspension". I've replaced it with "temporary leave of absence", as this seems to be a useful standard term that covers a great deal.'

'That's very considerate of you, Harry, and a great relief. I know that some people might want me to be knocked off my pedestal, but it would go too far if I was crushed underfoot.'

James stood up. He could feel the sweat forming and irritating his upper lip, but he must conceal his full feelings while Harry was present. He escorted him to the door, but there was something else that was a source of bother.

'Could you tell them, Harry, that I am preparing a report for Sir George Gribbins and that is why I am working from home? This is partly correct, as I do have to bring him in to the picture. Do you know if he has been involved in making this decision?'

James asked this casually, but it would be devastating if Sir George was involved in his suspension, or may even have initiated it.

'I have no idea. I think it came from local sources only.'

Elaine opened the door and saw Harry to his car. She could see that James was distressed and returned to see him in his favourite chair with his head in his hands.

'The bastards. They've suspended me – without any warning, without any explanation, without any opportunity for me to defend myself. I knew things were not going well, but to cast me off like this is intolerable. I'm seen as an embarrassment, a stain on the smooth running of the Poleaxe train, someone to be tossed off before the crowds greet it at its final destination. My presence equals offence, so I must disappear into the sidings.'

Elaine could only respond with empty reassurance, and this made him feel even worse. Then he realised the pavlova had been forgotten. The timer had already ended the fifty minutes. He checked the oven. The meringue was too hard. He smashed it on the table and stormed out.

Elaine tidied up and did her best to console him, but she made little progress. Her only success was to get him to agree to a short holiday away from all the troubles of Medenby. But, James insisted, only a short one, as this would bother Harry in his new role, but long enough to get the nasty taste of betrayal out of his system.

THIRTY-SIX

DAY ONE HUNDRED AND TWENTY-SIX

A wild creature is not subject to any will but its own

Jay Griffiths, 2008

The day had come. Carpe diem. Yes, it was ready to be seized and nobody would stop her. The day Barbara had thought about for years but which now appeared to be just another milestone on the expanding express route that was becoming Barbara's Way.

Pamela Dukinfield had great difficulty in letting go of her daughter. Barbara was now beginning to understand the reasons behind this and had done everything possible to make it easier for her. She made soothing noises about staying in touch by phone, every day at first until she was settled in the college residence, gave generous invitations for both her parents to visit at weekends – it was much more bearable when Dad came as well – and promised to come back home at least once a month.

'I honestly don't know how the church will do without

you, darling. You've been a permanent feature there for so long.'

'Permanent is not the right word, Mum. Everybody knew it was going to end at some point.' She stopped there, but she really wanted to add, 'You and they have taken advantage of me in every little corner of my life. Because you knew I could never say no, and would always feel guilty if I let people down, you piled on task after task on me, most of which I performed diligently and irritably, and then after each one I was covered in oleaginous praise, so sticky and offensive it made me want to vomit.'

So it was a great relief now to be able to smile sweetly and respond to every new request at church, 'I'm so sorry, but I'm going to be living at college now and unfortunately will not be available. I do hope you will find somebody else.'

And the problem with the church, and she guessed it was probably true of all churches now that the number of worshippers was falling, is that it was always on the take. Of course it could bless and forgive and pray, but the giving was abstract, almost metaphysical. 'Metaphysical' was a word that she had only just come across and liked playing around with. It was probably an important word, but it never seemed to go anywhere. Was it really concerned with the fundamental nature of existence, and of reality? She wanted to be convinced that the giving and taking at church were equivalent, but never could be quite persuaded that they were.

The taking was anything but metaphysical. The church was in need of repair, and even though the Methodist church was much more modest than its ostentatious

Anglican neighbour down the road, it still ate money. So there were raffles here, and flower arrangements there, and whist drives and bridge competitions, all to bring in extra cash. And whenever there were doubts, or when exhaustion was felt after a day's fundraising, the dreadful words, 'Never mind, it's all in a good cause,' would be uttered. It made many feel better. It always made Barbara feel worse.

It would be both a relief and an adventure to be living away from home. What a joy to be herself, unfettered. She would make mistakes, but she would own them. This was so much better than sharing in the errors of others. And she had started today with one major success already. Of course her parents wanted to take her to the student halls at the university. It was all female, and to Pamela Dukinfield that meant it was safe. No wild parties, no late-night drinking; good, honest supervision. But they wanted to see the halls for themselves, with Barbara in tow. They liked it and were looking forward to taking her there.

Barbara did not share these sentiments. Luckily, term started on a Monday, but students were required to come the day before, and Dad had to take the Sunday service. So, with some persuasion, Pamela and Robert had agreed to let Danny take Barbara instead, as he knew the university well from his own course in business management. He had recently bought a second-hand Austin A40 and was keen to show it off.

So, after a tearful farewell from Pamela and forty minutes of travel in Danny's chunky grey car, they arrived at the halls of residence. There it was, solid, well-built, with a soft, dark, comforting stone exterior and with balconies outside each of the rooms. She and Danny unloaded her cases, registered at reception and went up to the second floor. Barbara slowly turned the key and entered her new domain.

But this would not do. The bare, utilitarian kitchen, sitting room and bedroom were intolerably impersonal. Barbara had to work fast to make it into Dukinfield Corner.

So she opened the carrier bag, full of vegetables from the kitchen garden at home – it had been a good year, as more rain had fallen than usual – and stacked the carrots, leeks, potatoes, runner beans and beetroot in and around the kitchen. It was not important where they went at this stage; they just had to look right. Then she took out the thick folder with all the cuttings, pictures, drawings and photographs she had kept in her bedroom at home. Now she could display them.

So, with Danny's help, she taped them so they covered every blank wall in the sitting room and bedroom. The dresses that she wanted to wear, models wearing miniskirts (Mum had always disapproved of showing so much leg, but now she could wear them), dress patterns and drawings, and many prints of her favourite artist, Egon Schiele, especially his nudes, who all seemed to be telling an exciting but complicated story. It was so much better seeing them on a wall instead of having to be looked at surreptitiously at home.

When they had plastered every wall, Barbara was satisfied. But there was one other picture needed. She took out the small hammer from her bag and pinned a framed picture of some primitive statues above the bed.

Danny was intrigued. 'Now that's an interesting picture. What does that signify?'

'I'll tell you in a minute, but first of all you need to take your trousers off, just your outer trousers.'

Danny was puzzled but complied smartly. This was getting interesting. He sat on the bed, leant over, pushed Barbara down and started kissing her. She pushed him back up again. This was not yet the time for horizontal love-making.

'No, no, Danny, not yet. I've got to explain the picture first.'

She was using her schoolmarmy voice again. She went over and picked up a book from one of the cardboard boxes brought with them.

'This book is one of my anthropology texts. The picture above the wall is one of the unexplained mysteries of the subject. The statues, the Moai statues, in that picture are from Easter Island, a tiny island in the Pacific Ocean that was only discovered in the eighteenth century. The people who live there, the Rapa Nui, are Polynesians, but their ancestors, if they were indeed their ancestors, had all disappeared by the time it was discovered, probably died out.'

Danny was getting very aroused. He started to kiss her again.

'No, I haven't finished yet, and if we wait a bit it will be even better. The statues are made out of volcanic ash, easy to work but they are large and very heavy, and no-one knows how they were moved around. The trouble is, they left no written record, so nobody knows what these statues represent. So that's the puzzle. Each statue is different and they have faces that are very stern, almost as if they disapprove, apart from this one, who has a wry smile.'

She pointed at one of the statues in her picture. 'I'm very fond of this one and call him Mr M; he's my favourite Moai. I think he's one of your rivals.'

'You're talking in riddles, Barbara. Interesting riddles, but still riddles.'

'Now these statues, over eight hundred of them, all faced the village away from the sea. It looked as though they were protecting the community, but why should they need to do this? Were they meant to deter others or were they religious symbols?'

'As you're such a clever girl, I guess you have a theory.'

'Now you're making fun of me, but there is an idea I think we can look at together. Some people claim these statues represent phallocracy.'

'And what might that be when it's at home?'

'Danny, it's simple. Phallocracy is a society that is controlled by men.'

'That does not strike me as unusual. It's more or less universal. At least, that's what they tell me in management school. We only have three women on our course.'

'That's disgraceful, Danny. It has to change. Women are the best managers. They look after children. But there is a more literal meaning to phallocracy that people tend not to write about in our anthropology textbooks.'

'Of course I don't mind.' Danny wanted to kiss her again, but she stopped him. She was in control of this meeting and she did not want it to finish in the same way as the one with Stephen in his care.

'Please let me finish. The theory is that each one of these statues represents a phallus. And just so you never forget, a phallus is a penis.'

Danny looked at the photographs carefully. 'That's ridiculous, those statues are of faces.'

Barbara was very pleased that he was following her script. 'Now I am going to prove to you that you are wrong. But first you have to take off your underpants; you are looking uncomfortable down there. There we are, a big dome, below which is a ridge, and then a thick trunk, that seems to go right into the middle of your body. You are a perfect example of an Easter Island statue.'

Her plan was working perfectly. But she was still nervous about what would happen next. But Danny had no such concern, and in a few seconds her worry changed into craving. She removed her dress in one movement.

'It's clear to me you have all the credentials of a phallocracy, Danny Preston. Let's see if you can compete with Mr M, your rival.'

Barbara bent over and tossed him the silvery packet she had hid underneath the blanket. There were to be no hold-ups on this occasion.

'Remember, most of the Moai statues wore hats, so don't forget.'

A short time later, or it may have been an age, Danny went into the bathroom. Barbara lay on the bed, looking upwards in oozy contentment. A blank ceiling had never possessed so much meaning. And whether it was the powerful combination of Easter Island phallocracy, Danny's ardour and her own athletic enthusiasm, or just passion overcoming thought, her memory of the last few minutes – or was it hours? – was blurred. But the barrier she had contemplated for years had never existed. She had just passed through a gate. On the other side stood a girl; on this side stood a woman.

It was time for tea, and to sample the coffee cake that Mum had made for the occasion. Barbara and Danny looked at each other, a little sheepishly, as afternoon tea did not quite fit in with what had gone before.

'And what would Pamela Dukinfield be thinking if she knew about this?'

'It's very simple. You took advantage of an innocent girl and seduced me.'

Danny expressed mock horror. 'But what would she think if she really knew what happened?

'I hate to think. It would be along the lines of, "Where did I go wrong? When did my spotless daughter become a strumpet?" She might also blame anthropology, as to her it is full of primitive urges.'

They finished their tea. Danny looked as though he was about to go, but then he paused. 'You know, Miss Dukinfield. Your teaching has been most interesting and instructive. I think I would like to know more about Easter Island culture; it has lots of possibilities.'

Barbara grabbed his hand and pulled him towards the bedroom. Her clothes were already halfway off. They always seemed to get in the way on occasions like this.

'Come on, then, let's explore it together.'

THIRTY-SEVEN

DAY ONE HUNDRED AND THIRTY

No-one ever lacks a good reason for suicide

Cesare Pavese, 1950

There was a brisk wind blowing through the sand dunes as James parked his car close to the beach. The water was always warm at the end of August and the anticipation of being enveloped by it again pleased him. It was a relief to be away from all the troubles at Medenby. But he would have to return in the next few days and he must put this out of his mind.

Then the thought hit him. There was a way out of this mess. The aching rumblings that were churning in his head about his life, his work and his marriage could all be settled in a moment. Elaine was tough; she was already living a separate life and he was just a foot passenger. She would get a new partner quickly and could probably have children, as it was now clearer that investigations had shown that it was he, and not her, who was sub-fertile.

Now he was suspended from work, he could never return to his former optimism. The final rebuff came from Sir George Gribbins, who had just written to say that he had to support the suspension. He had added that he was sure it would come to nothing, but that was not the point. Why could he not have supported him when it was most needed?

The long-held belief that he could really make a difference to people's health was just a fond delusion, and now that all the stanchions holding him up had disappeared, he was bereft of all support. He, James, was the sole cause of all his ills. By staying alive he would drag others down with him; by dying he would release them all to a better future. The simplicity of this decision amazed him. Why had he not thought of it before?

He smiled as he thought about all those times in the emergency clinic when as a junior doctor he had persuaded desperate people to look to the future when they were suicidal.

'These feelings will not last,' he used to say to them. 'You are depressed. Depression is an illness. It is a disease with a very good outcome. You have to hang in there. You have good reasons to stay alive.'

Of course, he was not like them. He was not depressed. To be no longer alive was a logical consequence for him. His footprint on earth was never easy to detect; when it was removed altogether nobody would know. And in any case, he was not suicidal. He was just making a logical decision to disappear. Self-drowning was not self-slaughter; it was returning a body from whence it came.

But he must do it sensibly, with the minimum of fuss, and with little distress to others. So he turned round and walked to the telephone box at the end of the beach road. He got through to the guest house where he and Elaine had been staying.

Good, she was in her room.

'Darling, I'm just having a quick swim before coming home for dinner. The evening is too good to waste.'

'Of course, wish I could be with you. I'll get dinner organised for eight thirty. I'm sure you'll be ready for it.'

'Excellent.' James replaced the receiver. His voice had been firm and confident. She would never suspect.

There was no-one on the beach at this time as dusk had almost come. A few sanderlings were pecking indiscriminately in the sand at the water's edge, but clearly getting a good return from their efforts as they jerked and skittered in their twitching runs across the edge of the foam.

James smiled to himself as he stood for a few minutes watching the tide creep slowly up the beach. There was something calming about the certainty that every tenth or eleventh wave would creep a little further up the sand, leaving its shimmering trace for a few seconds before disappearing below. He retreated a little further, imagining that he was the conductor of this watery orchestra controlling its intricate moves. But of course he knew he was of no importance in this daily ritual. He could no more control the tides than King Canute, but it was nonetheless comforting to be a spectator on a part of life that he knew to be a certainty, one that was so far removed from his present turmoil.

Now only one thing remained. He stripped to his underpants, carefully folded his clothes, put them under a sea holly high up on the beach, and stepped into the water. His feet tingled as the waves lapped over them, almost inviting him in.

He walked slowly into the warm and comfortable sea, feeling as though with each step one barrier after another was being removed from his mind. Soon he was up to his waist and he was able to swim comfortably, slowly, towards the distant buoy in the estuary. A little further on he was out of his depth and he swam further into the twilight caressed by the waves. There was only the dreamy lapping of water of his face and shoulders disturbing the peace of the lovely evening.

The next day the crab fishermen were out early. They noticed something in the water.

'Another dead seal,' said one.

'No, it ain't, it's a body,' said the other.

They pulled over and lifted the creamy white form into the back of the boat.

'Yet another one getting out of his depth in a riptide – should be more warning signs on the beach.'

But before they covered James with a tarpaulin, they could not help looking at his face and noticing his serene smile. This was not a man who had died in distress, or were they deceived, you could never really tell. But there was no time to think. They must get the body back and have it reported before they continued on the important tasks of their day. Crabs were still in high demand.

THIRTY-EIGHT

DAY ONE HUNDRED AND FORTY

Smart lad, to slip bedtimes away
From fields where glory does not stay
And early though the laurel grows
It withers quicker than the rose

AE Housman, 1896

They had decided to have James's funeral in the old parish church just south of Medenby. It was six hundred years old and had a famous Easter sepulchre carving that visitors came for miles to see. James was no churchgoer, but his wife Elaine had been in the past and her father was buried in the graveyard there. As so many people wanted to remember him, the church was an obvious choice. It was just outside the Medenby exclusion zone and now the barriers had been removed it was an opportunity to recapture their travelling freedom.

Barbara felt she had to go to the funeral as it was connected to the Poleaxe story, and she now felt it was her story too. She knew about James, and his fall from grace, and although she had only seen him briefly when she was in Block G, she had always been troubled by him. He was always on edge, looking truculent, with darting looks like a suspicious fox on the prowl. It was sad that he had drowned while swimming, but she was curious to know what had really happened.

The mourners had begun to arrive. They were greeted at the porch by a smiling churchwarden and beckoned in. Barbara realised she would not recognise most of the people coming and so hung about at the rear, only going into the church when a bigger crowd had arrived, allowing her to blend in and become anonymous. She saw William Fothergill and Dr Merridew, the neurologist, in one of the front pews, so realised she was at the right funeral.

Then, just before the service began, she saw James's family arrive. That neat-looking slim woman must be James's widow, Elaine. She was obviously distressed and was helped into the church by an older couple. They must be James's parents. They were troubled too, but in a sad way, not an agitated one. But there were no children and apparently no brothers and sisters, so James must have been an only child. Barbara could sympathise. His parents had lost their only son; what a tragedy for them.

The pews were uncomfortably bare and there was no heating. Barbara looked around. She could see little optimism in the old mediaeval pillars, the sepia and grey church walls, and the silent sorrowers, but her spirits were lifted by the curvilinear east window, with its wild tangled stonework and brighter sky beyond.

The Reverend Roy Deacon took the service. He had been well versed in advance and had taken his responsibilities seriously. He outlined the story of James's life, his determination to become a doctor and make a difference in the world, his happy marriage, his work in public health and his tremendous commitment to the work of controlling the Poleaxe Syndrome, that had led to him reaching the peak of his career.

Roy spoke slowly and as his voice was penetrating, nobody in the church could avoid hearing every word. He paused just after intoning the words 'tremendous commitment' and Barbara heard a woman say 'yes, yes, yes' close to her. It was clear that James Porton had inspired much affection. He was not a man who would be forgotten easily.

The hymns were sung, ending with William Blake's 'Jerusalem'. Whenever Barbara heard the first few bars of the hymn, she tingled all over. It always raised her soul, and she was able to join in with genuine elation.

After the service Barbara was keen to get away quickly. The church was impressive and more imposing than the Methodist church at home, but the day had begun dull, and all the mourners seemed miserable and out of sorts. But, she had to remind herself, this was a funeral, not a celebration, so she must not be too harsh.

But as she walked away she heard a woman come alongside her. 'So you're Barbara Dukinfield, aren't you?'

This was not a friendly voice, but Barbara could not deny her name. She turned towards a large middle-aged woman in a green beret and matching coat.

'You're the one who's been causing all this trouble over Poleaxe, aren't you?'

'I'm not at all sure I know what you mean.'

'Come off it, young lady. You're the one who helped that psychiatrist and that Dr Camberwell.'

'And how do you know about that?'

'I worked for Dr Porton, so I know all about your little tricks. Making out this Poleaxe Syndrome was all mental. You ought to be ashamed of yourself.'

'I have no idea what you are talking about. I suffered from the Poleaxe Syndrome and answered questions that I was asked as a patient.'

'Don't play all innocent with me, you little minx. It was you who gave all these fancy ideas to the doctors about anxiety. You, who haven't got any qualifications or experience, taking it upon yourself to tell the world how important you are.'

Barbara had tolerated this for long enough. 'I've no idea who you are and what you are trying to say. But something I can conclude is that you are amazingly rude and ignorant. I have acted in good faith and been honest with all. I have not pushed my views on anyone. You are clearly upset about Dr Porton, but there is no need to take it out on me.'

She immediately turned on her heel and marched off so swiftly there was no opportunity for any response. Within seconds she was out on the road and striding back into town. Walking quickly helped her to control her anger but also helped to suppress her tears. She was not used to being insulted and whether or not it was justified was unimportant. It was upsetting and bad for her self-confidence, and it made her peevish.

Although she did not regret coming to the funeral this contretemps had shown her perfectly that stigma was alive and thriving in Medenby. If she had helped to find the bug that caused Poleaxe she would be lionised and praised universally. But because she, Stephen and Giles had found a contributory factor, possibly a cause, that was mental, not physical, they were reviled as interfering scandal-mongers whose only intention was to sabotage the investigation. Four centuries ago she would probably be regarded as a witch and burnt at the stake. But had understanding of illness changed much in that time? It certainly had for physical illness but seemed to have come to a full stop for mental disorders.

But the conversation had made one thing clear. She was in the middle of the Poleaxe controversy and could not escape. Her only option was to go forward.

THIRTY-NINE

DAY ONE HUNDRED AND SIXTY-NINE

A man should look for what is,
and not for what he thinks should be

Albert Einstein, 1949

Barbara had managed to get a pass to the press conference where the final verdict on Poleaxe would be presented to the world. Giles had managed, by a combination of guile and persuasion, to get a pass, as six places had been reserved for the people from Medenby involved in the Poleaxe Task Group. Not all of them had been taken up. William Fothergill had decided not to come and, of course, James Porton was absent also. Stephen was not well enough to attend either, so Giles was able to persuade the organisers that Barbara was 'Dr Bollider's deputy' without indicating she had no medical qualifications.

Barbara sat with Giles at the back of the large hall.

'The two people sitting behind the table are Kenneth Robinson, the Minister of Health, and Sir George Gribbins,

236

the Chief Medical Officer,' whispered Giles. 'It's good that Kenneth Robinson is there because he's very interested in mental health, so he'll be a champion for you.'

Barbara was only partly reassured.

The minister introduced himself and Sir George. Barbara thought his voice was soft and friendly, and it encouraged her.

'We will host this meeting about the Poleaxe Syndrome in two parts, as it is a complicated subject. The first part is the public health one. We want to assure the population of these islands that they need to have no further concerns about this unpleasant condition. The second part is mainly for the science and medical journalists gathered here, and is concerned with the cause and implications of the syndrome. Sir George, who has been intimately involved with the history and development of Poleaxe, will now summarise the public health position.'

Sir George rose. Barbara was impressed with his presence and great height; he would certainly hold everyone's attention. But was there something wrong with his eyes, and did he have a monocle? It did not really matter. She sat back in her chair and waited in considerable anticipation. Would her work be mentioned? Giles has already told her not to be too optimistic.

'Poleaxe is a disease that has taken much disentangling. It appeared suddenly in the town of Medenby and appeared to be a completely new condition. It paralysed the limbs, fortunately only temporarily in most cases, but sadly was fatal in others. It also turned out to be infectious, so it quickly spread. Through the valiant efforts of Dr James Porton, Medical Officer of Health for Medenby, who sadly is no longer with us following his death in an accident, the disease was contained by quarantining Medenby from the rest of the country. This was very effective in containing the disease and the number of cases has steadily reduced since, and there have been none in the past two weeks.'

Barbara was concerned. There was no mental health component mentioned yet.

'After detailed enquiry and exhaustive research, the cause of Poleaxe has been found to be a virus transmitted by a tick. This tick, to the best of our knowledge, is only found in the Cameron Highlands of Malaysia and the person carrying the virus to Medenby had visited the forests there shortly before leaving Malaysia.

'The virus, once in the body, creates an illness like a mild dose of flu and is infectious. This is why so many other people in Medenby became infected too. The most serious consequence of infection is sudden paralysis of the arms and legs, hence the common term "Poleaxe".'

Barbara was getting increasingly concerned that mental health might be squeezed out of this summary. It needed to be in national newspapers tomorrow.

'The public health physicians noted early on that many people exposed to the virus did not get the Poleaxe Syndrome. This is unusual, as we normally expect resistance from people already exposed to the disease, but to the best of our knowledge this is a new disease. But here the cause of the resistance was different. People who were constitutionally calm were immune from the neurotoxic – that is to say, the paralysing – effects of the virus, but those who were highly nervous and anxious were susceptible. We have now a full set of data, analysed by a national anxiety expert, Dr Malcolm Loader from the Institute of Psychiatry here in London and by Dr Leo Gibbons at the University of Newcastle, that shows that of nearly three hundred people with the Poleaxe Syndrome, ninety-five per cent had abnormally high scores on anxiety questionnaires, had high blood cortisol levels and strong anxiety predispositions. Put another way, they were anxious before they were exposed to the virus.

'Research by Dr Giles Camberwell in Medenby, who I think is in the audience today, has shown that if anxiety levels are reduced by giving a sedative drug such as diazepam, commonly known as Valium, to people with the Poleaxe Syndrome, the paralysis is relieved, only to return again when anxiety levels rise again.'

Barbara turned and smiled at Giles. Her natural smile was now an incandescent one. Sir George had said what they both wanted to hear, in simple, straightforward language that nobody could fail to follow.

'We are now confident that the Poleaxe epidemic is over. The virus does not live long in the body and after three to four weeks it is gone. We therefore expect no more cases. But we need to understand more about this curious and alarming syndrome. After questions we will move to the second part of this press conference that will explain our plans to make sure we do not succumb again.' Sir George sat down, seemingly in some relief.

Kenneth Robinson took over. 'We now have a short time for questions before moving on. I should say before we start that I am glad that we now have better understanding of how mind and body join together to create disease. For those, like me, who are trying to put mental illness higher on our national health agenda, this is a very positive development.'

Questions followed. It was not surprising that most of them focused on Sir George's conclusion that the epidemic was over.

'How can we be confident that Poleaxe won't occur again?' asked a waspish reporter from the *Daily Mail*. 'You had no clue when it arrived. How can you be so confident it has gone?'

Sir George remained urbane. 'You are very welcome to stay for the second part of this meeting if you wish, as our reasons for saying this will be explained. If you want a simple military analogy, Poleaxe is defeated because our army is stronger and we have infiltrated its lines. All the possible ways of Poleaxe returning have been anticipated.'

The other questions were ones of clarification. Many of the journalists left and the second part of the meeting began. Barbara was now leaning forward with greater interest. This was where she would be learning something new.

Kenneth Robinson was on his feet again. 'We had to split this meeting into two parts because of its complexity. I am no doctor, but I am a campaigner for mental illness. We still think of illnesses as either mental or physical, with no overlap between them, and where there is an overlap we think that one follows the other, or vice versa. What Sir George will now explain is how Poleaxe shows these two elements are joined together. I hope you can follow his arguments; I've had three lessons already but I think I now understand.'

There were a few giggles for Kenneth seeming to act as an earnest schoolboy.

Sir George stood up again. 'I said earlier we now know the virus is caused by a tick, *Haemaphysalis cameronii*. I don't need you to remember this, except to remind you that ticks live off the blood of animals, mainly mammals. This particular tick is probably a new species – the Natural History Museum tells me – and is found only in the Cameron Highlands of Malaysia.'

Barbara tingled all over. So she was right.

'Although this tick species is new to science, it must have been present in Malaysia, at the very least in the Cameron Highlands, for many years. So we would have expected that the Poleaxe Syndrome would have been identified before in that part of the world as it is such a prominent disease. The reason why it has not is directly related to the mental aspect of the syndrome. The native people of the Cameron Highlands, the Senoi tribe, are very jealous of their tribal area and very few people go there. What we have found, for reasons that are not yet fully known, is that the Senoi tribe are constitutionally non-anxious.'

Barbara wanted to shout out, 'It's their dreams, there's your answer,' but of course could not. She was only there as an interloper and might have been escorted out for shouting such apparent nonsense.

'Because they are universally calm, when members of the Senoi tribe get bitten by a virus-affected tick, they develop a brief respiratory illness only, never Poleaxe. We came across a similar phenomenon in Medenby. Our public health colleagues came across many people who had been exposed to the virus but had not developed Poleaxe. These were people with low anxiety levels. So colleagues at Imperial College in London investigated this further with

241

blood samples from people who had been exposed but not developed the syndrome, and compared these with those who had. They found that the virus multiplied when in the presence of high anxiety hormone levels – for those who are interested, the main ones were catecholamines and prolactin – but was at least partly deactivated when these hormone levels were low.

'So in terms of causation we can say that the Poleaxe Syndrome is a neurotoxic condition occurring in those with anxious dispositions but not in others. It is a genuine psychosomatic disorder; both elements need to be present for it to be manifest.

'Our plan now is threefold. With the help of the Malaysian government, we will try to eradicate this tick from what is a relatively small area. We also will issue warnings to all travellers about the potential dangers of the Cameron Highlands as a holiday destination. Thirdly, we intend to make the reduction of anxiety a major public health strategy in this country. This is supported strongly by the Ministry of Health and we hope shortly to have a new Royal College of Psychiatrists who will be able to spearhead this initiative.'

Sir George sat down and was replaced by Kenneth again. 'I would like to reinforce the last point made by Sir George. For too long have we relegated mental health to the backwaters of the NHS. Aneurin Bevan reminded us that a good health service is one "where rich and poor are treated alike, that poverty is not a disability, and wealth is not advantaged". Those with mental illness are still the poor who are not treated alike, and for whom there is poverty of treatment and where wealth does advantage. We must do all we can to reverse this, and the Poleaxe story must end with a promise that we can and must do more.'

A burst of applause followed this stirring finale. There was no need for questions. The message was absolutely clear, and even though many might forget it easily, it would still remain.

As the room emptied, Giles turned towards Barbara. 'Game, set and match to Barbara Dukinfield, I should say.'

'Don't be silly, Giles. I'm just a pawn on the chessboard.'

But of course Barbara was extremely pleased. She kept remembering what her grandfather said to her just before he died: 'Whatever you do in life, Barbara, ask yourself at the end, *Did I make a difference?*'

She could now answer, 'Yes.'

FORTY

DAY THREE HUNRED AND EIGHTY

*ich nun Selber einer von Denen bin, die mit dieser traurigen
Affection behaftet sind, und mir die Thatsache der Vererbung
schon frühzeifig klar war*
*(I am now myself suffering from this sad disease and early
recognised it was heritable.)*

Julius Thomsen, in the scientific paper in which he first described
the neuromuscular condition that would in time be named after him,
Thomsen disease, 1876

The headquarters of the Royal College of Physicians in
London was celebrating its third anniversary. The many
delegates of all ages streamed towards the award-winning
cantilevered concrete building jutting proudly and
resplendent in the morning sunlight. They were doctors,
some young and callow, others knowingly self-important
at the peak of their careers, and a smaller group, who
were slower, some stooped and limping, but showing that
retirement had not blunted their need for knowledge.

244

They were all coming to the annual meeting, where new discoveries would be presented and awards for achievement given.

Barbara too was walking with Danny among the others in the park, sensuously feeling the sunshine caressing her face and neck as they strolled, overtaken by the doctors and some commuters anxious to get to their many destinations. As she walked she was trying to fathom if she loved Danny or if he was just a special friend. She adored being with him, she would hate it if he left her life, he was fantastic as a sexual partner and he was a great companion. But did all this amount to love? And was he the only one? Amy had suggested she should 'play the field', but when she found out what this meant it just seemed like promiscuity, one of the anathematic words of Methodism. In the end she had decided that as she was only twenty, there was still time to solve one of the mysteries of her personal universe.

She looked at him again. Part of her just wanted to put her arm round Danny, wrestle him down to the inciting warm grass and explore him intimately for the rest of the day. This at least would be uncomplicated. But of course that would involve tearing up a page in the Pamela Dukinfield Book of Etiquette – not in public, never on display.

In any case, she was puzzled. Danny had suggested she had a break from her studies and a visit to London Zoo would make it a special one. She was flattered and agreed. But the next day he had mentioned an event at the Royal College that might be of interest to her anthropology studies. He would not explain further, saying it would mean more if it was kept a secret.

So she, somewhat self-consciously as one of the few women entering the building, soon found herself with Danny in the Great Hall. She was bemused. Whatever else was going on here, it had absolutely no connection with London Zoo. She sat near the back, partly for anonymity, but also to look at the others in the hall.

'What has all this got to do with me?' she whispered to Danny.

'Wait, it will all become clear,' he said, patting her elegant knee, and letting it rest a little longer than it needed to. 'You may meet some old friends.'

She settled down and looked around the auditorium. It was a strange sight. Most of the people were men, half of them in white coats, obviously doctors, all looking very serious and studious, some with notebooks. Obviously this was an educational event, not a jamboree. This was certainly not her familiar territory, but it was interesting. And she felt pretty calm. Yes, that was worth noting. A year ago this place would have made her want to run away or hide in a corner. And it was not just Danny beside her that made her more settled. Even though she really had no right to be here, she did not feel out of place, as she too was a student of higher learning.

And who was that down in the front row? Yes, their backs were turned, but she recognised them both, Giles and Stephen. And Stephen was sitting alert and upright; he must have recovered. That was a real pleasure. So that was the reason Danny had fixed up this meeting. She squeezed his hand and nodded in the direction of the two at the front to show she understood.

The gentle hubbub of conversation was dying down. A man in a resplendent gown walked down the aisle and mounted the stage. Danny showed Barbara the programme. This was Sir Ian Moregill, President of the College. He stood at the dais and waited until there was absolute silence. Barbara imagined herself in the same position, except in her case silence would probably never come. Sir Ian must have presence, or perhaps the gown provided it for him.

'Today we are, for the first time, celebrating the achievements of the younger generation of doctors. We have not forgotten the old, but all too many of them receive their accolades many years after their discoveries, often so long afterwards,' he paused briefly, 'they have forgotten what their awards were for.'

A delicate titter rippled across the hall.

'Praise and recognition means so much more for the young. They can be emboldened and reinforced, driven on to even better things. So we at the Royal College want to encourage the exuberance and novelty of youth by recognising their talents early, not when they are old and grey.'

Sir Ian continued, and before long reached the climax of the session.

'So now we are able to present our major award, Young Doctor of the Year. Our panel had no difficulty in choosing this one. We are not often faced with a new disease within the shores of our islands and the Poleaxe Syndrome has taxed our ingenuity to the limit. Valuable insights, and excellent preventive measures, were provided by James Porton, who unfortunately is no longer with us. But the breakthrough that allowed us to find the cause of the disease, the elusive tick carrying the anxiety-sensitive virus,

Haemaphysalis cameronii, came from Stephen Bollider and Giles Camberwell. The enterovirus is transmitted by tick bites and leads to paralysis of the limbs. Many of those affected do not have symptoms as the virus is inactivated in the presence of normal catecholamine levels. But in those with high plasma catecholamines, the virus multiplies and becomes neurotoxic. The paralysis is reversible if catecholamine levels can be reduced within four hours.

'So, together, Stephen and Giles have demonstrated to us the first truly psychosomatic disease, one in which both mental and physical causes are intertwined as intimately as the molecules of DNA. The story of their discoveries is already appearing in the learned journals but must also receive proper acknowledgment from our college. Come forward, Stephen Bollider and Giles Camberwell, Young Doctors of the Year.'

Both Giles and Stephen came up the steps to the podium, Giles with a little more agility than James. They were presented with their awards. Barbara peered from a distance; she could not wait to see exactly what they were.

Giles came to the microphone. 'But, Sir Ian, you may have omitted a much more important person who is really deserving of this prize. This person, not a doctor, not even a health professional, is the one who is the most worthy of distinction. She is an anthropologist, and has the advantage over us of understanding culture and context in illness. It is she who, after being one of the first sufferers of the syndrome, pointed the way towards the elucidation of this unique disease, and without her we would have been nowhere. To put it briefly, it was she who first noticed that anxiety was a strong component of the disease, it was she who demonstrated that anxiety made the disease worse if you were already infected, and it was she who first pointed the finger at the Cameron Highlands as the source of the virus.'

He paused for effect.

'The final coup de grace delivered by Barbara was the explanation for the curious absence of the Poleaxe Syndrome from historical and current records. How had it been hidden all these years? It was Barbara who noted that the Senoi tribe in the Cameron Highlands were almost universally calm. Why? Because their lives were predicted by their culture, the culture of sharing all their dreams. This removed worry and uncertainty from everybody and so, when infected, the Poleaxe virus gave them only mild respiratory infections, never muscular paralysis. So I am sure that you would agree, Sir Ian, that it would be appropriate for Barbara Dukinfield to be invited to the stage.'

Barbara was temporarily transfixed. She was recapitulating her awareness of first recovering consciousness after Poleaxe. Unreal, bizarre, detached, yet peculiarly contented. Somehow she found her way to the podium. Sir Ian had been forewarned. He confirmed that Barbara had indeed been the key to discovery of Poleaxe, and then he paused. It was not clear if he had finished or not.

But then he added, 'Ladies and gentlemen, I am sure that you would agree that we also need to be encouraging more women to join our college and promote our research. So, to encourage the others, as it were, we have decided to create a special prize for Barbara. She cannot, of course, have a young doctor's prize but instead we are promoting her in a different way. We are first suggesting that the Poleaxe Syndrome be renamed. Now that it is no longer the demon we feared, it needs a new name. It should now be called Dukinfield Disease, after its main discoverer. And I would like to mark this occasion with a special memento for Barbara.'

He stepped forward and gave Barbara a glass figurine of a prostrate figure with 'Dukinfield' etched on its base. She stared at it in bemusement but then did what she always did when overcome with emotion; she disappeared into his gown and hugged him. He did not seem to mind.

The audience was a little bemused by this strange turn of events. But then realisation seeped in. A few people started clapping, and once begun, the applause spread incrementally, like a giant wave breaking on a pebbly shore, raising a few cries of 'Bravo' on the way, until it reached a crescendo. Barbara soaked it in. To be thanked for doing something that she never expected to become known was the best of accolades. But, a far, far better result was that she was now poised, assured and certain of herself. The future lay before her like a magic carpet. She just had to climb on.

Acknowledgements

I thank Sue Bailey, for plugging parity of esteem against all odds; Swaran Singh, for introducing me to the twilight unconscious; Ben Spears, for reminders of the past; Heather Cameron and Colin Godber, for parental insights; Philip Macdonald and Robert Sloan, for helping me understand how Methodists party; Catherine Gardiner, for ebullient optimism; Christian Gold, for German lessons; Ian Gilmore, for letting me misspell; Simon Wessely, for his skills in avoiding becoming a main character; my wife, Helen, for her help in moving me from evidence-based to creative writing; and the Nightingale nurses of St Thomas's Hospital in the 1960s for showing me the true components of good care. Finally, Shelley Weiner, Nidhi Arora, Ursula Brunetti, Lola Coker, Eileen Phillips, Vicki Howard, Grace Maxted, Larry Wallace and all the others from the Faber Academy course of 2018–19 deserve special appreciation for showing that whatever else appears in novels, it is the quality of the writing that really counts.